Enjoy th
Mh

MW00880064

THE BOX M GANG

MARK L. REDMOND

Contents

CHAPTER 1

When I found Pa lying on the stable floor one morning, I knew he was dead before I rolled him over. Doc Greenwood had told us almost a year ago that something was wrong with Pa's heart. Pa hadn't looked or acted sick, so we had reckoned the problem must not have been too serious. Sitting with my back against one of the stalls, I began planning what to do next.

I reckon most folks believe that a fifteen-year-old girl ought to cry when one of her parents dies, and I did cry when Ma passed. In fact, I couldn't stop crying. Two years later I still cried whenever I thought about her.

But as I sat there looking at Pa, I felt no sadness; I shed no tears. I had loved him because he was my father. I had never liked him. Pa had been a hard man. He had driven Ma and his five children instead of leading us. There had been no tenderness in him toward any of us. Ma told me once that fighting in the war had changed him, but I always reckoned she had just been trying to justify his behavior.

"He's dead, ain't he, Ruth?"

I jumped at the sound of Thad's voice. He had entered the stable silently, walking the way Pa had taught him. He had paused just inside the door, but then he glided to the stall and sat beside me. He put his arm around my shoulders, and neither of us spoke for a while. Finally, Thad broke the silence.

"I reckon you should tell the young'uns," he said. I always smiled when Thad referred to our younger sister and two brothers as "the young'uns" because they weren't much younger than the two of us. "We don't want them coming out here and seeing Pa like this. I'll dig a grave beside Ma's."

"Maybe you should come to the house with me before you do any digging," I said. "Let's tell the others together. I reckon we need to talk about a few things."

Thad gave me a curious look, but he helped me to my feet and followed me to the house. Although I was a year older than Thad, I had never tried to boss him around. We had always been friends.

The five of us gathered around the large oak table in the kitchen. Billy and Bart sat across from me. "Where's the grub?" asked Billy. "I'm hungry." I smiled. Like most eight-year-old boys, Billy was always hungry. I reckon that was why he was nearly as big as Bart, who was two years older.

"Where's Pa?" asked Bart.

"He went to the stable," said Sarah. At twelve, she was often mistaken for my twin or even—to her delight—my older sister. "I'll tell him to wash and come to breakfast." She pushed her chair back and started toward the door.

"Wait!" I said. Sarah looked over her shoulder at me but kept walking.

"Why?" she asked. Glancing at the stove, she grinned. "Well, I declare, Ruthie Martin! You haven't prepared our breakfast yet! What have you been doing that was so important that you neglected your duties? Pa isn't going to be happy about this when I—"

"Sit down, Sarah!" I said.

"You're not the boss of me!" she said. Sarah opened the door.

"Pa's not coming to breakfast," I said, "today or ever again."

Sarah closed the door, tip-toed back to the table, and sat beside me. Staring at the table, she reached to take my hand. "What do you mean?" she whispered.

"Did Pa run away?" Billy asked.

"Last year Johnny Davis ran away to join the army," said Bart.

"Did Pa run away to join the army?" Billy asked.

"No," I said, "Pa died." Then, not because of losing Pa, but because of the hurt I saw in those three faces, I cried.

Billy and Bart cried too; but Thad and Sarah just sat, staring at the table. Nobody spoke for a while.

Billy had leaned forward on the table and buried his face in his arms. He startled the rest of us when he sat up and wailed, "We're orphans! The sheriff's going to take us to the orphan house!"

Getting Billy to settle down took some time. Thad built a fire in the stove, and I made us some flapjacks for breakfast. As I worked, I planned.

We ate in silence. When everyone but Billy had finished, I began to share my plan.

"If we all work together," I said, "I think we can stay here instead of going to the orphanage."

"Billy's right," Sarah said. "As soon as folks find out Pa's dead, the sheriff will come out here with a buckboard and haul us to the orphanage."

Billy started wailing again. "We're going to the orphan house!"

After we had settled Billy down for the second time, I started over. "If we all work together," I said, "I think we can stay here."

"We can't stay here now that Pa's gone," Thad said. "Sarah's right; as soon as folks find out, the sheriff will come for us."

Billy opened his mouth and covered his eyes.

"Stop, Billy!" I said. "Don't you start fussing again until you hear me out." I looked around the table at what was left of my family.

"Sarah is right; once the town folks find out that Pa's gone, they'll want to put us in the orphanage. That's why we're going to make sure they *don't* find out."

Four mouths dropped open. I couldn't keep from smiling just a little.

"Think about it," I said. "Pa doesn't have to be alive to keep us out of the orphanage; folks just have to *think* he's alive. If we work together, we can keep this place going without him."

I looked at Thad. "To start with," I said, "we need to bury Pa where no one will see his grave. Burying him next to Ma would spill the beans."

Billy whimpered, "Beans is all they feed them orphans at the orphan house."

"Bart, you and Billy get dressed, and tend to the livestock," I said. "Sarah, clear the table, and wash the dishes. Give Thad and me an hour, and then bring the boys to that stand of cottonwoods by the swimming hole."

Sarah shoved her chair back and stood with her hands on her hips. She sneered and shook her head.

"You are not the boss of me," she said. "Just because Pa is gone—"

"Fine," I said. "Just pack a carpet bag with whatever you want to take to the orphanage. We don't want the sheriff to have to wait when he brings the buckboard to haul us away."

I pushed my chair in, turned, and walked toward the door. With my hand on the latch, I said, "Thad, if we're going to the orphanage, we don't need to hide Pa's grave. I reckon we can just bury him beside Ma and save ourselves some trouble."

"No, wait!" Sarah said. "I'm sorry! I'll clear the table and wash the dishes. You and Thad bury Pa near the cottonwoods."

When I turned to look at Sarah, she was pale; and her hands were clasped in front of her. I smiled and nodded at her.

"Thank you, Sarah," I said. "I don't know if we can get away with what we're planning or not. I do know that our only hope will come through all of us working together."

"I'll hitch the roan to the wagon and get a couple shovels," Thad said. "The cottonwoods are too far away for us to carry Pa."

"I'm coming too," I said. "Sarah, we'll see you and the boys in about an hour. Please bring Ma's Bible with you."

As I followed Thad outside and pulled the door closed behind me, the sun warmed my face. Birds were calling to each other, and a bee buzzed past my head. We neared the stable, and I smelled the familiar odors of our livestock. Everything around me seemed as it should be, but I shuddered. I had never been more afraid.

CHAPTER 2

By the time Sarah and the boys joined us under the cottonwoods near our spring-fed swimming hole, Thad and I had buried Pa. Both of us were panting and sweating as we leaned on our shovel handles.

Sarah handed Ma's Bible to me. As we stood in a circle around the grave, the boys removed their hats; and Sarah bowed her head. I read Psalm 23, thinking more about how it applied to our lives than how it had anything to do with the way Pa had lived.

As we started back toward the house, Sarah took my hand. A few steps ahead of us, Thad sat between Billy and Bart on the wagon seat. By the time Sarah and I walked into the yard, Thad and the boys had unhitched the roan and put her in the corral. We entered the house without speaking. I walked to the table, laid Ma's Bible on it, pulled out a chair, and sat.

The five of us sat at the table in silence, not looking at each other. The only sound was Billy's occasional soft whimpering. After what must have been a quarter of an hour, Sarah spoke.

"What are we going to do, Ruth?" All four of them looked at me.

"We're going to do exactly what we have been doing," I said. "Each of us will do the same chores and have the same responsibilities he had yesterday or last week or last month."

"Who's going to do Pa's work?" Thad asked.

"You and I will have to divide that between us," I said. I couldn't sit still any longer. I scooted my chair away from the table and stood. "I reckon we have a couple things that will help us pull the wool over other folks' eyes."

"What other folks?" asked Bart.

"How much of our wool will that take?" asked Billy. He began to cry. "You promised me a new blanket."

I slid my chair back under the table. Resting my hands on the back of the chair, I rolled my eyes at Thad. He was trying not to grin.

"What I meant," I said, "is that we have a couple things that will help us keep folks from finding out that Pa's—" I looked at Billy. "That Pa's gone."

"What things?" Sarah asked.

"Well, for one thing," I said, "Pa hadn't really been doing a lot of work around here since Ma died. Folks who stop by from time to time are used to seeing us working the ranch, so they won't be suspicious."

"What if someone wants to know where Pa is?" Bart asked. "We ain't supposed to lie."

"We *aren't* supposed to lie," I said.

"Ain't that what I just said?" Bart asked.

I smiled. "I reckon it is," I said. "We won't lie to them; we'll distract them and avoid giving them a direct answer."

"What do you mean?" Bart asked.

"I'll show you," I said. "Pretend you're a rider who just stopped by and found me gathering eggs."

"In the house?" Billy asked.

"No, Billy," I said. "I'd be inside the fence around the chicken coop." I looked at Bart. "Ask me about Pa."

"I know about Pa," he said.

"You're supposed to be a rider who stopped by," Sarah said.

"What's my name?" he asked.

"Your name is Bob," Sarah said. "Ask Ruth about Pa."

Bart squinted at me and spoke in the deepest voice he could. "Howdy, little Missy. Is your pa around?"

I smiled at him. "I reckon he's not here right now," I said. "I don't expect him back tonight."

Bart was grinning. "That wasn't lying," he said.

"What's the other thing that will help us?" Thad asked.

"Look around," I said. "We're in the middle of nowhere. This ranch is a good ten miles from our nearest neighbor, and almost three times that far from Tucson. We see two, maybe three riders in a month. Nobody's paying any attention to us, so we won't have many folks to fool."

"You're right about that," Thad said, "but we still need to keep on our toes when someone does come around."

"How will that help?" Billy asked. "Are we going to try to look taller?"

"No, silly Billy," Bart said, "we're going to try to be quiet—you know—sneak around on our tip-toes."

This time Thad rolled his eyes at me. "I reckon we're going to need a lot of help from God if we're going to make this plan work," he said.

"I reckon we are," I said. "We're also going to need a lot of time to teach these two how to act when we have company."

Bart sprang from his chair and banged his fist on the table. "We're not babies!" he said. "Billy and me know how to act around company, don't we, Billy?"

"Yes," Billy said. His lower lip was quivering. "Don't talk with your mouth full. Don't pick your nose. Don't interrupt when grownups is talking. Don't wipe your nose or your mouth on your sleeve—"

"You're right, Bart," I said. "You and Billy aren't babies. Billy, you're right too. The things you mentioned are important whether we have company or not."

"Then what are you talking about?" Bart asked. He unclenched his fist and sat down.

I pulled out my chair and sat for a minute or two without speaking. As I studied their faces, I thought about how much I loved my family. I folded my hands and swallowed the lump in my throat.

"We're fixin' to try something that most folks would say is impossible," I said, "and maybe it is. One slip of the tongue could land us all in the orphanage." I looked at Billy. "Don't cry, Billy. Let me explain what I meant about teaching you and Bart how to act when we have company."

"This isn't just important for the young'uns," Thad said. "All of us need to be careful about what we say and do."

"You're right," I said. "What I'd like to do to get us ready for company is to practice—to play games. We need to pretend we're company and ask questions like folks who stop by will ask."

Sarah smiled. "If we make mistakes talking to each other, it won't matter, will it?"

"No, it won't," I said, "but it will show us where to be careful and how to answer the questions other folks ask us."

"When do you think the first rider will stop?" Bart asked.

"Maybe a month from now," I said.

"Or maybe tomorrow," Thad said.

"What are we going to do?" Bart asked.

"Let's take care of our chores first," I said. "By the time you're finished, I'll have supper ready. We can start practicing while we eat."

"You didn't tell them about our plan did you?" said Mirza.

"Well, not exactly. I mean, they knew we were going to do a recce. I just didn't…"

Mitch shook his head. "You're out of control."

"Hey, it was a good plan. We played the cards we were dealt and it worked out for the best."

"Yeah, well now I'm pretty keen to play my hand with that bell-end, Pershing," said Mitch.

"Me too," added Mirza.

"That makes three of us."

CHAPTER 36

EL PASO, TEXAS

Christina placed her few belongings into a plastic bag and walked out of the hospital. It was late afternoon and she had spent the better part of the day waiting for the doctors to approve her release. Finally, a handsome young resident had handed her a box of antibiotics and signed the necessary document. It was not until she looked at the box on her way out that she realized he'd scribbled his phone number on it.

She squinted as she stepped out into the sunshine.

"Where do you think you're going, miss?"

There he was, leaning against a signpost with his battered Yankees cap pulled low. "Aden!" She blushed as she realized how excited she sounded.

"There's a diner around the corner. You mind if I buy you a coffee?"

She hugged him. "Sure thing."

"What was the last thing you remembered?" he asked as they walked.

"You saving my life. I've got a faint memory of another man being there. Dark, angular features, some kind of doctor."

He chuckled. "A doctor, he'll like that."

"So who was he?"

"A friend from work."

"From the UN?"

They arrived at the diner and sat at the only curbside table.

"Yeah. I told him where we were going and when I missed a check-in he got in contact with Emilio."

"OK. And Roberto?" she asked hesitantly.

Aden took off his hat and rubbed at his temples. She noticed the flecks of gray and the bags under his eyes.

"We rescued him yesterday. He sends his regards. Wanted me to tell you that you're welcome to visit when things settle

CHAPTER 3

Our ranch was only 240 acres, a little southwest of a settlement called Green Valley, Arizona Territory, and about 30 miles south of Tucson. I reckon Pa had chosen that property because he had known the soil there was rich enough to grow food for both his family and his livestock. We got more rain than most of the territory, and we never seemed to be too hot or too cold.

I couldn't remember a time when our family had possessed an abundance of anything, but we had always seemed to have enough of the things that are necessary. I reckoned there were two reasons for that. One reason was that Pa was careful with what little money he had. The other reason was that Pa worked harder than anyone else I have ever known.

Both of those reasons had stopped being a part of Pa the day we buried Ma. The meanness had remained, but I had never seen him do a lick of work around the ranch again unless he had to. If he had any money, neither Thad nor I had seen it.

Our livestock consisted of one longhorn bull and twenty cows, one stallion and twelve mares, a ram and five ewes, and a flock of twenty-some chickens that included at least four roosters. Although our animals steadily produced offspring, the herds had stayed about the same size.

Pa had made his money by selling our older cattle and an occasional horse. Sometimes the buyers were folks who rode past our ranch and wanted to replace livestock they had lost along the trail. Most of the stock Pa sold to folks from Green Valley. Twice each year, he'd cut out two or three cows and a horse and head for Green Valley. He usually returned the next day.

The calves and foals born in our herds replaced the stock Pa sold. That was the reason the size of our herds didn't change much. The number of sheep and chickens stayed about the same because we used them for food when we couldn't get deer or antelope.

While I was thinking about these things, I prepared our supper. Since I had helped Ma for most of my life, cooking came easy to me. I had been doing all the cooking since Ma had first gotten sick. That part of our new life would remain the same.

"Whatever you cooked sure smells good!" Bart said.

"It's chicken and dumplings," I said. "Did all of you wash up?"

I was standing at one end of the table, holding the last of the five bowls I had filled. I set the bowl on the table and smiled at Thad. We bowed our heads.

"Thank you for this food, Lord," Thad said. "Please guide and bless us. Amen."

"Amen," the rest of us said.

As usual, we ate without talking. I had taken two or three bites when I noticed that Billy wasn't eating. He grinned at me and tipped his bowl to show me that it was empty.

"Billy!" I said. "How did you eat that so fast?"

Still grinning, Billy said, "You don't even have to chew these dumplings! They just slide right down to your belly!"

When we had stopped laughing enough for me to speak, I explained to Billy that chewing needed to be part of eating dumplings. After the rest of us had finished eating, all three boys asked for second helpings. Sarah and I waited while they ate, and then we put cups, bowls, and spoons into a washtub full of water to soak. We returned to the table and sat.

"I reckon the key to making our plan work," I said, "is going to be us telling ourselves every day that someone is watching us."

"Ain't God watching us all the time?" Billy asked.

"*Isn't* God watching us," I said.

"That's what I'm asking you," Billy said.

I took a deep breath and looked at Thad. He was grinning. "Yes, Billy," I said, "but I'm talking about behaving as if other folks are watching us."

"What other folks?" Billy asked.

"Folks who happen to ride past the ranch, Billy," said Bart. He opened his eyes as wide as he could and smiled at Billy. "And folks who hide in the brush to watch us."

"Bartholomew!" I said. "If Billy can't sleep tonight, you're sitting up with him."

Billy's lower lip was trembling. "Are folks hiding in the brush to watch us?" he asked.

"No," Thad said. "Bart was just teasing you."

"What I was trying to tell you," I said, "is that if we always act like someone is watching, we'll be doing what we're supposed to do whenever someone actually comes calling."

"That makes all kinds of sense," Sarah said. "We don't ever have real company. Most folks who stop are either looking for food and water or asking for directions."

"And if some folks did want to rest their horses and spend the night," Thad said, "they'd sleep in their wagon out by the stable."

"They would," I said. "Nobody will be paying much attention to us. The dangerous time will come if someone wants to talk to Pa."

"We can decide what to do about that when it happens, can't we?" Sarah asked.

"I reckon not," Thad said. He looked at me. "Ruth?"

I shook my head. "We need to have answers ready before someone asks about Pa," I said. "We want to be honest, but we can't raise folks' suspicions."

"I don't understand," Bart said. "What do you mean?"

I pushed my chair away from the table, stood, and held out my hand toward Thad. "Let's show them what I'm talking about," I said.

Thad pushed away from the table, stood, and walked toward the door. Sarah gave me a confused look.

"Where's he going?" she asked.

"I have no idea," I said.

Thad opened the door, looked at me over his shoulder, and grinned. "I reckon we ought to make this look real for the young'uns," he said. Stepping outside, he closed the door behind him.

Bart and Sarah were grinning and watching the door. Billy wiped his eyes with his sleeve. "Is Thad running away?" he asked.

"No, silly Billy," Sarah said. "He's pretending to be a stranger. Watch."

When Thad knocked on the door, I opened it and let him in. He glanced around the room as if he'd never seen it before, nodded toward the table, and then smiled at me. He spoke in a deep voice.

"Howdy, Ma'am," he said.

"Good morning, Sir," I said. I bit my lip to keep from laughing at him.

"I was hoping I could speak to your husband, Ma'am," he said.

"Thad!" I said. "I'm only fifteen years old! I don't have a husband."

Thad squinted at me. "I'm a stranger. I don't know how old you are. Some girls marry young."

I held up my hands. "You're right," I said. I took a deep breath.

"I'm not married, Sir," I said. "My sister and brothers and I live here with our pa."

"I beg your pardon, Ma'am," Thad said. He was using his deep voice again. "May I speak with your father?"

Before I could answer, Billy started sobbing. "Pa's dead, Mister, and we buried him down by the swimming hole. We—"

"Billy!" I said. "We can't tell people that Pa's dead! Just listen." I turned to face Thad.

"Pa's not here right now," I said. "Maybe we can help you."

Thad looked at the ceiling and took a deep breath. Then he grinned at me.

"My family and I are travelling to Phoenix," he said, "and one of our horses pulled up lame three days ago. I was hoping you folks might have a horse I could buy from you."

I glanced at Sarah and the boys. They sat, wide-eyed and open-mouthed, waiting for my answer.

"I reckon we have one or two Pa would be willing to sell," I said. "Let me show them to you and see what you think."

Thad and I turned toward the table. He bowed, and I curtsied. We returned to the table and sat.

Bart leaned forward, staring at me. "You can't sell our horses without asking—" he looked around the table, "somebody."

"The horses are ours," I said. "So are the cows, the sheep, and the chickens. Thad and I will decide which animals we can sell and which ones we should keep."

"What about the bull?" Billy asked.

"We'll keep the bull," Thad said.

"What about the roosters?" Billy asked.

"We'll keep them too," I said.

"What about Bart?" Billy asked.

"We'll only sell him if we get really short on food," I said.

Billy laughed. Bart started laughing, and then we were all laughing. We laughed for several minutes, and the laughter felt really good.

CHAPTER 4

Pa had died near the end of January. February passed quietly for us secret orphans. We followed the same routine each day, just the way we had when Pa was still with us. Each of us had certain chores to do, and we did them. Well, most of the time, we did them. Once in a while, I had to remind somebody.

One evening when we sat down for supper, Billy looked confused.

"Hey, Ruth," he said, "I didn't get any food!"

"You're right," I said. "Neither did the chickens."

Billy stared at the table. "I forgot to feed them," he said.

"And I forgot to feed you," I said. "I reckon I'll remember by the time you get back to the table."

Billy looked at me. His lower lip trembled, and he brushed away a tear with his sleeve. He pushed his chair away from the table and shuffled toward the door. With his hand on the latch, he looked over his shoulder. Between sobs, he said, "I'm real hungry, Ruth."

I took a deep breath. "So are the chickens," I said. "You can eat as soon as you've fed them."

No one spoke as I walked to the stove. I loaded Billy's plate with beef and beans. When I turned and started back toward the table, I found three pairs of eyes fixed on me.

"You're mean!" Bart said.

"No, Bart," Thad said. "Ruth is right." He leaned forward, one elbow on the table, bringing his face closer to Bart's. "What if Ruth had forgotten to cook dinner for us? What if Sarah had forgotten to wash our clothes? What if Billy had forgotten to gather the eggs or you had forgotten to milk the cow? What if you had forgotten to fill the water trough for the sheep?"

"I understand," Bart said. "I'm sorry, Ruth. I reckon you weren't being mean. If we don't do our chores, they won't get done."

When Billy came in a few minutes later, I was waiting at the door to give him a hug. I knew he had washed his hands, because he was wiping them on his shirt as he started toward the table. Before he had reached it, he stopped and looked at each of us.

"I'm sorry for not feeding the chickens," he said. "I won't forget again."

"We'll help you remember," Sarah said, "and we'll remind each other too. We all forget things once in a while."

Billy smiled as he scooted up to the table and began to eat. "Then I reckon I'll remind you too," he said.

The next morning, as usual, we left the house just after sunrise, ready to begin our daily chores. I saddled our bay mare so I could ride out to check on our livestock. I led the mare from the stable and paused to look around me. Sarah was scrubbing our clothes in a wooden tub. Bart was milking the cow. Billy was gathering eggs in the chicken pen. Thad was replacing a broken post in the corral fence. Everything looked the way it should on the Box M Ranch.

I smiled as I mounted the horse and started her toward the pasture. The sun was shining; the morning air was cool and fresh. The day would be beautiful. I had just started to hum an old hymn when I spotted the buzzards.

Now, I know that buzzards have a purpose, just like most of God's other creatures. Ma had told me one time that if buzzards didn't clean up dead animals, the whole world would stink. I believed her, but I still felt a little sick whenever I saw those nasty birds circling over something dead or dying.

These buzzards were already flying low, and they were dropping rapidly. When I realized they had to be flying over our pasture, I nudged the mare to a gallop. As I approached the pasture, I slowed her to a walk, rode to the gate, and reached down to let myself in.

At first, everything looked as it should. The cattle were spread over one end of the pasture, grazing on the grama grass that grew between scattered junipers and other bushes. I thanked God when I saw that our bull was among the cattle, alive and well. A few of the cows looked at me and then went back to eating. I rode toward the far side of the pasture until I could see the ground along the fence. I turned the mare away from the cattle, riding close enough to the fence that I wouldn't miss anything. Glancing up at the buzzards, I saw that I was headed toward the center of their circle.

I smelled the dead steer before I saw it. I reckoned that a cougar or a rattler might have killed it. We had lost cattle to both of those no-good critters in the past. When the mare started getting skittish, I knew I was close. I pulled my bandanna over my mouth and nose, stood in the stirrups, and watched the ground ahead.

I tried to prepare myself for the sight of a bloated carcass if the cow had been snake-bitten, or a half-eaten carcass if it had been killed by a cougar. When I found it a few minutes later, I gasped because I had not prepared myself for the sight of a cow that had been killed and butchered.

I rode to the gate, left the pasture, and closed the gate behind me. The first of the buzzards landed beside the carcass as the mare passed the corner fence post.

Although I knew there were plenty of rustlers in the Arizona Territory, none of them had ever bothered the Box M before. Any rustlers I'd heard of had always driven stolen stock away from the ranch then butchered or sold them. Why had someone killed and butchered a cow in the pasture and risked being caught red-handed? I shuddered. Had someone been watching us long enough to learn our daily routine? Did the rustlers know when we usually checked the pasture? Did they know Pa was dead? Were they watching us now?

I dismounted in front of the stable and wrapped the mare's reins around a hitching rail. Sarah was hanging the laundry on the clothesline. Bart and Billy were cleaning the stalls with a pitchfork and a wheelbarrow. Thad had finished replacing the post and was walking from the corral to the stable, carrying a pick and a shovel. When he looked at me, I nodded toward the house.

A few minutes later, Thad stepped into the house and closed the door behind him. He took off his hat and wiped his sleeve across his forehead.

"What's wrong?" he asked.

"Let's sit," I said. I had put two cups of water on the table, and we drank before I spoke. "We lost a cow, probably yesterday afternoon," I said.

"A break in the fence?" Thad asked.

"No," I said. "It was dead."

"Aww!" he said. He banged his fist on the table and shook his head. "Cougar or rattler?"

"Rustlers," I said. "Somebody butchered it right there in the pasture. The buzzards led me to the carcass."

Thad ran his hand over his face and let out a long breath. He closed his eyes for a few seconds, then looked at me.

"It might have been someone just passing by," he said, "but I don't reckon it's very likely that a drifter would have found our herd."

"No," I said, "it's not." I drank more water. "I reckon whoever butchered that cow wasn't too worried about being interrupted."

"Because he knew where we were?" Thad asked. He sloshed the water around in his cup.

"More than likely," I said.

"Then whoever it is has been watching us," he said. He finished his water and stood.

"Where are you going?" I asked. Thad walked through the doorway to the parlor. When he returned, he carried Pa's Winchester rifle.

"I'm going to see if I can find whoever killed our cow," he said. "If we let him get away with killing one cow, I reckon he'll think nothing of killing another one. It's not like we can tell the sheriff, Ruth. Remember, he's the man who'll take us to the orphan home."

I sprang from my chair, almost knocking it over, and grabbed Thad's arm. "Wait!" I said. "What will you do if you find the rustler, or rustlers? I reckon there's a good chance at least two varmints were in on this business, and maybe even three."

"I'll try running them off our land," Thad said, "after they pay us for the cow they killed." He tapped the rifle. "I reckon this should help me persuade them to pay up and light a shuck out of here."

I shook my head. "That should work just fine if the rustlers are little girls with no weapons." It was my turn to visit the parlor. I crossed the room and lifted the heavy double-barreled shotgun from the gun rack. I broke open the breach and shoved a brass shell into each barrel. After snapping the breach shut, I grabbed four more shells from the box on the shelf and crammed two into each of my pockets.

Thad's eyes widened when I stomped back into the kitchen. "You figure you're coming with me?" he asked.

"You figure you'll try to stop me?" I asked.

He grinned. "I reckon I won't while you're holding that scattergun," he said.

CHAPTER 5

Thad hung the rifle by looping its leather strap around the saddle horn. Then he swung into the saddle and pulled me up behind him on the mare. Neither of us wanted to waste time saddling a second horse. Since the mare was young and strong, Thad let her gallop until we could see the cattle. A few buzzards still circled low above the cow's carcass, but most of them were busy feeding.

Thad reined the mare to a stop about twenty yards from the gate, and we dismounted. Standing still, he studied the area around the gate. He pointed toward some tracks that led toward us.

"I reckon these tracks are yours," he said. I followed him as he walked toward the gate. When he had covered a little more than half the distance, Thad stopped. He pointed in the same direction we had been riding. "These tracks are the ones we need to follow."

This time Thad held the mare to a walk. As we rode, both of us watched, listened, and sniffed the gentle breeze that blew against our faces. We were searching for anything that didn't belong. Although I couldn't see the tracks we were following, I knew Thad could. I lost track of time; but, judging by the sun's position, I reckoned we had been riding for at least an hour.

We had seen, heard, and smelled the things that belonged around us: antelope, coyotes, mule deer, prairie dogs, sage, hawks, quail, and a few more buzzards. Then something in my mind recognized a faint smell—something that, while it was familiar, was out of place.

"Thad," I whispered, "do you smell it?"

He stopped the mare and took a deep breath. "Someone's cooking beef!" he said.

I closed my eyes and inhaled the breeze. "I smell coffee too," I said. "What are we going to do now?"

Thad dismounted and waited for me to join him. "We're going to take a closer look," he whispered. "Follow me."

Since Pa had trained all our horses to be "ground hitched," we weren't worried about the mare wandering off while we were gone. After both of us had taken a good drink from our large canteen, Thad poured water into his hat and let the mare drink too. Both of us checked our weapons, and I patted my pockets to make sure the extra ammunition was still there.

The ground we had crossed since leaving the pasture was rolling, covered with juniper trees and enough brush to provide plenty of places for a man on foot to conceal himself. There were some places where a horse could hide too. I didn't reckon our cattle rustlers were too concerned about hiding since they didn't expect anyone to come after them.

Although I had just taken a drink and the day wasn't a hot one, my mouth felt desert dry as Thad and I walked up the rise in front of us. The smell of cooking beef and coffee grew stronger as we neared the crest of the hill. At the first sound of talking and laughter, we dropped to the ground. Although I couldn't understand the conversation, I thought I recognized at least three voices.

My heart pounded as we crawled the next four or five yards. I glanced to my left as Thad dropped to his belly. Following his example, I used my elbows to drag my body forward a few inches at a time. A large greasewood bush gave us both cover as we stretched our necks to look at the ground that lay below.

With one exception, the downward slope looked much like the one we had just climbed. The difference on the side we now viewed was the fire at the bottom of the slope. Three men sat cross-legged on the ground around it. A large steak sizzled in an iron frying pan that sat on the fire, and a coffee pot rested on a flat rock at the fire's edge. As we watched, one of the men drew his belt knife, used it to turn the steak over, wiped the blade on his pants, and returned it to its sheath.

A tin plate and a fork sat on the ground beside each rustler. The men drank coffee and talked as they waited for the steak to finish cooking.

"I reckon if we ride out at sunup, we can take our time," said one of the rustlers. We couldn't tell who had spoken because two of the men wore their hats. The third man's sombrero hung on his back from a stampede string, but he sat with his back toward us.

"We'll pick a spot toward the top of that long grade I told you about," said the same man. "The stage will be crawlin' along nice and slow. Some of the passengers might even be walkin' up the hill beside it. That's when we'll take it."

The sombrero man put on one of his leather gloves and removed the frying pan from the fire. With his other hand, he drew the knife he had used earlier, set the frying pan on the ground, and sliced the steak into three pieces.

With his fork, he put meat on the plates his two companions held out to him. Then he set the frying pan aside and put the last piece of meat on his own plate.

Thad nudged me with his elbow; and when I looked at him, he pointed over his shoulder. When we had crawled a safe distance from the crest, he whispered, "What should we do?"

"I don't know," I said. I could feel a knot in my stomach. "They plan to leave in the morning; maybe we should ride back to the ranch and just let them go."

Thad scowled. "Have you forgotten whose beef they're eating?" he asked.

"Keep your voice down!" I said. "It's only one cow. Is it worth risking our lives for one cow?"

"Those cows *are* our lives, Ruth!" Thad said. "We can't afford to let hombres like these three steal our cattle. If we do, others will steal from us too."

As much as I hated to admit it, I knew he was right. I took a deep breath and let it out slowly. "Lord, help us," I said.

I reckoned Thad's plan was a good one; but as he laid it out, the knot in my stomach tightened. When he had finished, he stood, took my hand, and helped me to my feet. My knees felt weak, and Thad must have seen my fear in my eyes. He hugged me and whispered in my ear, "We have God on our side, Ruth."

I kept repeating his words as I worked my way in a wide circle toward the rustlers' camp. I had wanted to stay together, but Thad had insisted that approaching from both sides was the best way to get the drop on the men and to disarm them. He had also insisted that we needed to remain unseen for as long as possible. He reckoned the rustlers would be more likely to give up their weapons if they didn't know we were young'uns.

We were downwind from the rustlers' mounts and their packhorse, but still I crept through the brush on my hands and knees for what must have been close to an hour. My leather gloves and my canvas pants had protected me from the rough ground; but sweat dripped from my nose and my chin when I peeked around some brush to check the rustlers' camp.

At first, I saw no sign of them. When I lifted my hands from the ground and stretched my neck like a giant prairie dog, I saw that all three rustlers were asleep on their blankets. I didn't realize that I had been holding my breath until I blew it out between my nearly closed lips. My heart was pounding. Although I knew what was about to happen, I still jumped and covered my mouth with my left hand when Thad spoke.

"Hello, the camp!" he yelled from the brush.

All three rustlers sat up, holding their six-guns.

"You're surrounded," Thad said, "so toss your guns toward me and stand up nice and slow."

Scared as I was, I smiled and whispered, "*slowly, Thad.*"

While the outlaws stood, trying to find Thad in the brush, I crawled as close as I dared get to them and waited for Thad's next command. We had reckoned that those polecats wouldn't believe they were surrounded without some kind of proof. We were right.

"I reckon you're out there alone," one of the rustler's said, "or you'd show yourself."

Without turning his head, he said, "Boys, he can't get all three of us before we get him. Let's rush him."

"I reckon your dumb pardner might be right, Boys," Thad said. He was enjoying this too much. "I might only get one of you. I want to be sure I get the right one. I need you to do two things for me. First, I need whoever wants to be dead first to raise his hand. When you rush me, I don't want to get excited and shoot the wrong man."

The three men looked at each other, but no one spoke. Suddenly I realized what Thad was doing. He was trying to spook these rustlers so that we'd have an edge.

"You said you needed us to do *two* things," the dumb one said. "What's the second one?"

"I need you to take three steps to your right," Thad said.

"Why?" asked the dumb one.

"So that you don't get hurt," Thad said.

This time they mumbled something to each other, but they moved to their right. I pulled back one hammer on the shotgun. I almost felt sorry for them, but then I remembered what they had done to our cow.

"Coffee pot!" Thad said.

I'm a good shot, but I reckon almost anyone could have hit that coffee pot from where I was hidden. All three men had their backs to me. I raised up enough to get a clear shot, pressed the stock against my shoulder, and squeezed the trigger. That 12-gauge shotgun let out a roar. I ducked as soon as I had fired, but I could still see what happened in the camp.

That coffee pot sailed about ten feet into the air, turning end-over-end and spewing coffee in every direction. When it landed on the ground, rolling to a stop twenty feet from the fire, it looked more like a sieve than a coffee pot.

All three rustlers had jumped when I fired. One ducked, grabbing for his empty holster.

The second one sprawled face down in the dust. The dumb one spun while he was in the air and landed, feet wide apart and facing my direction. I stayed hidden as I broke the shotgun open, removed the empty shell, replaced it with a loaded one, snapped the shotgun closed, and tucked the empty shell into my pocket. In spite of our situation, I smiled.

From somewhere close behind me, a deep voice spoke. "Be still, Miss. I don't aim to hurt you." The man reached over my shoulder and took my shotgun. "Let me hold this while we talk. Now that you and your brother have done such a good job of capturing these outlaws, what do you reckon you'll do with them?"

CHAPTER 6

My heart hammered as I tried to catch my breath, and my stomach felt sick. I had been kneeling behind a bush, keeping my head down while I put the empty shotgun shell into my pocket. I reckoned the sound of my shot might have covered some of the noise the man behind me would have made as he approached. I also reckoned my attention had been focused on the rustlers and their coffee pot while this man was sneaking up behind me. Still, he had been able to move close to me without my knowing he was there. I didn't know anyone besides Thad who could have done that.

Taking a deep breath, I turned, still on my knees, to face him. I expected to find myself looking into the barrel of the man's gun. Instead, I found myself looking into his big brown eyes and his dark brown smiling face.

The man sat cross-legged on the ground about six or seven feet from me with my shotgun lying across his lap. He wore fringed buckskin coat and britches along with knee-high buckskin moccasins. He had removed his wide-brimmed leather hat and laid it on top of the shotgun. His bald head glistened with sweat. He removed his brown bandanna, wiped his head, and tied the bandanna around his neck again. He was still smiling. When he spoke, his voice was deep and gentle.

"Please forgive me for scaring you like that, Missy," he said. "After watching you shoot that coffee pot and then reload your gun, I reckoned we might have a more pleasant conversation if I held it till we was better acquainted. My name is Jeremiah Jackson, but my friends call me Jem."

"Are we friends?" I asked. My heart and my stomach had almost returned to normal. The man certainly didn't seem threatening.

"I'd be obliged if we could be, Miss—uh, Miss—"

"Ruth," I said, "Ruth Martin." I smiled at him. "I reckon maybe we could be friends, Jem."

Still smiling, he leaned forward and held out his large right hand. "I'm pleased to meet you, Miss Ruth."

We shook hands. Jem handed me the shotgun, put on his hat, and stood. Reaching down with that big right hand, he helped me to my feet and waited while I brushed the dust from my knees.

"Let me fetch my horses," he said. "I'll be right back." He turned around and walked away without making a sound. As I watched Jem disappear behind a pile of rocks, my head began to clear. I liked Jem, but what did I know about him? Could I trust him? He walked from behind the rocks, leading a buckskin and bay pack horse toward me. What was he doing on our property? I needed some answers. After he had stopped his horses in front of me, I got them.

When he held out his canteen, I realized I was thirsty. I swallowed some of the warm water and handed the canteen back to him. He took a drink, corked the canteen, and looped the leather strap over his saddle horn. He looked at me and smiled.

"I reckon you have a few questions to ask me," he said. "Could we walk toward the rustlers' camp and your pardner while we talk? Those men won't stand there much longer without making some kind of a play. If we let them make it, somebody will most likely get hurt or killed."

"Can you stop them?" I asked.

Jem stopped his horse and patted its neck. He opened a saddlebag, reached into it, and pulled out a pair of iron handcuffs. "I reckon I can, Miss Ruth," he said. "These irons usually make men behave themselves, and I have a pair for each of them." He slipped the handcuffs back into the saddlebag, and we started walking again.

"These three hombres have committed worse crimes than rustling your cattle," he said. "They're wanted for stage and bank robbery as well as murder. I've been tracking them for almost two weeks. But they had a big lead when I started."

This time I stopped. "Thad and I heard them planning another stage robbery!" I said. I started walking a little faster than I had been. Without looking at Jem, I asked, "Are you a lawman?"

"I do the same work that a lawman does," he said.

"You're a bounty hunter?" I asked.

"Yes, Ma'am, I am," he said. "We can continue our conversation after we secure these outlaws. I'd suggest that you point your shotgun in their direction. I reckon you can encourage them to mind their manners while I put these irons on them. You can ask your pardner to join us too if you want."

The three rustlers hadn't moved from where they had been standing, but they had lowered their hands. Seeing Jem and me, they raised their hands again.

When they realized that I was the one carrying the shotgun, they looked surprised. The one in the middle started to lower his hands. "What the—"

"I reckon you'll want to keep your hands up, Mister," Jem said. "Remember what this young lady did to your coffee pot."

Scowling, the rustler shoved his hands into the air. "I should have known better than to take up with you two no good—"

"Shut your mouth, Jake!" said the man on his left. "In case you ain't noticed, your hands is raised too. Some boss you turned out to be!" He spat on the ground close to Jake. "You let us get taken by a little girl and a N—"

"I don't care much for that word," Jem said. He hadn't raised his voice, but he had drawn his six-gun. "Besides, she didn't need my help to catch the likes of you three. I just offered to help her deliver your smelly carcasses to the law."

Jake was still scowling. "So, you expect us to believe that wasn't you giving orders from the brush behind us?"

Still holding his gun, Jem pointed over his shoulder with the thumb of his left hand. "I rode in from that direction, and you three had already tossed your guns away."

The rustlers glanced at each other. The man on Jake's left leaned forward a little and asked, "Then who was hiding in the brush behind us?"

"I was," Thad said.

All three men jumped at the sound of Thad's voice, and they turned their heads to look at him. Jake muttered a curse.

"Another kid!" he said.

"Jem," I said, "meet my little brother Thad."

Jem was grinning. "That boy moves like a ghost," he said. He holstered his gun and waved his right hand. "I'm pleased to meet you, Thad! You can call me Jem. I have handcuffs for your prisoners—leg irons too if you want them."

Thad looked at Jem, then at me. I nodded and shrugged my shoulders.

"I'd be obliged for your help," Thad said.

Jem looked at me and smiled. "Let's shackle us some outlaws!"

Thad kept his rifle pointed at the rustlers while Jem shackled their hands behind their backs. After he had shackled them, he searched each man and removed tobacco, folding knives, and money from their pockets. He put everything into a cloth sack and tied it shut with a short piece of twine. As he worked, he told Thad most of what he had told me half an hour earlier.

When he had finished, he surprised Thad and me with a question. "Well, what do you want to do with these hombres?"

Thad and I looked at each other. Thad removed his hat, ran his fingers through his thick, brown hair, and then replaced his hat. He looked at the rustlers.

"They stole one of our cows," he said. "They need to pay us for it."

"I reckon they do," Jem said. He removed his hat and bandana, wiped the sweat from his head, replaced his hat, and spread his bandanna over a bush to dry. "How much was the cow worth?" he asked.

Again, Thad and I looked at each other. I motioned to Thad.

"I reckon Pa usually got somewhere around twenty-five dollars when he sold a cow," he said.

47

"Has your pa stopped selling cows?" Jem asked.

After glancing at me, Thad said, "Pa has stopped doing everything. He died."

Jem removed his hat again. "I'm sorry," he said. He looked as if he really meant it. "What about your ma?" he asked.

"She died a couple years ago," I said.

Jem shook his head slowly. He put his hat back on and let out a deep breath. "Do you want to be paid in gold or paper money?" he asked. He was still holding the sack that contained the rustlers' belongings.

"Pa always asked for gold," I said.

"Then gold it is," Jem said. He put one big hand into the sack and felt around. When he withdrew his hand, he held a fifty-dollar gold coin. Tossing it to Thad, he said, "This should cover the price of the cow and pay you both wages for the day you had to waste trying to catch these hombres."

Neither Thad nor I could speak. Jem grinned when he saw the look on our faces.

"Who would have thought that these three would be so generous?" he asked. His expression became serious.

"I'd like to make a suggestion," he said. "Could we ride to your house, fasten these three to something so they can't escape, and then sit down to discuss their future?"

After getting a nod from Thad, I said, "We can. Thad and I have a younger sister and two brothers that have to be wondering what has happened to us. I'll prepare some food and coffee, and we can talk after we eat."

"That sounds real good!" Jem said. "I'll get these hombres packed up and ready to go."

"We'll give you a hand," Thad said.

Something like a quarter of an hour later, Thad and I rode the bay mare toward the ranch house, followed by Jem and the three rustlers.

CHAPTER 7

"I can't recall the last time I had such delicious venison stew, Miss Ruth," Jem said.

All of us had finished eating except for Billy and Bart, who had divided the last of the stew between them. Bart was soaking up the broth with a piece of flatbread while Billy drank the last of his broth from the bowl.

"Billy," I said, "remember your manners!"

"Sorry," Billy said. Setting his bowl on the table, he patted his lips with his napkin and grinned. "How's that?" he asked.

I closed my eyes and let my breath out slowly. I didn't see who laughed first, but all of us ended up laughing. When we stopped laughing, Sarah excused herself and began to clear the table, putting the dishes in the washtub. I reminded Bart and Billy that they needed to finish their chores before they went fishing or did whatever else they had planned for the afternoon.

The day was beautiful, so Thad, Jem, and I walked outside. The porch was shaded from the afternoon sun. I sat in one of the rocking chairs Pa had made, and Thad motioned Jem to the other. Then he seated himself on one of the two-person benches Pa had also built.

Thad and Jem had chained the rustlers to one of the posts that supported the stable roof. Before chaining them, we had freed their hands to let them eat some of the stolen beef they had cooked to take with them on the trail.

"Would you mind if I smoke my pipe while we talk?" Jem asked.

"Not at all," I replied. Pa had smoked a pipe, and I had always liked the smell of his tobacco.

"Why don't you tell me as much about your family as you can—or as much as you want to," Jem said. He pulled a short-stemmed pipe and a tobacco pouch from a leather bag that hung over his shoulder on a strap. While he packed his pipe, placed it between his teeth, and lit it, I began to tell him the important parts of our family's history. He listened with his eyes closed, smoking his pipe and rocking slowly. He didn't speak until I had finished talking and looked at Thad.

"I don't reckon you left out anything that matters," Thad said.

Jem stood, stepped to the edge of the porch, and knocked the ashes from his pipe. Then he put the pipe into his bag and returned to the rocker. He folded his arms across his broad chest and looked at us.

"If I understand you right," he said, "nobody knows that you five—" he paused, looking for the right word.

"Young folks," I said.

"You five young folks," he said, "are living here, running this ranch without your Ma and Pa. You can't turn these rustlers over to the sheriff because he might discover your secret and put you in an orphanage."

Thad and I looked at each other, then at Jem. "Yes, Sir," Thad said.

Jem leaned forward, his hands folded and his elbows resting on his thighs. "I've been following these hombres because there's a bounty on them," he said. "I planned to capture them, take them to Tucson, and collect the bounty."

"Can't you still do that?" I asked.

"I can," he said, "but only on one condition."

Confused, I looked at Thad; but his expression told me that he didn't understand either.

"What condition?" he asked.

"When the territorial marshal locks those three in jail and pays me," Jem said, "y'all get half the reward money."

Thad stood; and when he spoke, he voiced my thoughts as well as his own. He spoke with respect, but he was firm. "We're obliged for your offer, Sir, but we Martins don't accept charity."

Leaning back in the chair and smiling, Jem raised both hands until they were even with the brim of his hat. "I don't recall offering you any charity," he said. "I'm talking about wages. I trailed those men to your ranch; but the first time I laid eyes on them, they had empty holsters and their hands in the air. Y'all captured them, and I'm taking them to Tucson. Where I come from, we call that a partnership."

Thad sat down again, looking at Jem. "I—I don't know what to say," he said.

Jem, still smiling, held out his right hand. "Do we have a deal, Pardners?" he asked.

After both of us had shaken hands with Jem, Thad replied, "I reckon we do, Pardner."

"Then I reckon I'll hit the trail with my herd around sunup tomorrow," Jem said.

"I can have breakfast ready before you leave," I said. I stood and looked toward the stable. "I can feed those three too. Will you eat with us?"

Jem stood too and took off his hat. "Miss Ruth," he said, "I never did claim to be the smartest hombre in the territory, but I reckon I'm too smart to pass up an offer like that." He replaced his hat. "I'd be obliged to have breakfast with you—if it won't be too much trouble."

While we worked at our chores that afternoon, Jem checked the shoes on his own horses and the four that belonged to the outlaws. Then, after asking Thad for permission, he checked the shoes on our three shod horses too. He had just finished replacing a nail in one of the bay mare's rear shoes when I walked into the stable with one of our canteens.

Jem stood and stretched his back muscles. He accepted the canteen, took two sips from it, and handed it back to me.

"I'm obliged, Miss Ruth," he said. I followed him out of the stable and watched as he removed his bandanna and soaked it in the horse trough. He wiped his head and face, rinsed the bandanna, and tied it around his neck. "I have a favor to ask of you and Thad," he said.

We walked to the corral. Jem lifted his hat from the top of a post and put it on his head. He leaned on the fence rail and nodded toward where the rustlers' horses stood in a bunch.

"One of the reasons I'm good at what I do," he said, "is that I don't let anything distract me. In my business, distractions can get a man killed." He brushed a fly away from his face. "Those three hombres we caught have had plenty of time to make a plan to escape before I can get them to Tucson. They'll be waiting for me to get distracted; then they'll jump me."

Again, I offered him the canteen. He took a long drink, replaced the cork, and handed the canteen back to me. He pointed at the horses.

"I always travel with my own pack horse," he said. "A second pack horse would only be a distraction that I don't need." Jem looked at me. "I'd be obliged if you and your brother would keep that bay pack horse."

Jem must have guessed that I was about refuse his offer. Before I could speak, he smiled.

"You'd be making my job easier and making the trip safer for me," he said.

"Let me check with Thad," I said.

"About what?" Thad asked.

Both Jem and I jumped when Thad spoke. When we turned to face him, Jem's gun was in his hand.

"Thaddeus Martin!" I said. "What have I told you about sneaking up on folks?" I took a deep breath and let it out slowly.

Thad stood still, his hands in the air. He was staring at Jem's six-gun. "I wasn't sneaking," he said. "I was just walking."

Jem lowered the hammer on his gun and slid it into his holster. He shook his head slowly and grinned. "I'm sorry, Pardner," he said. "You do move like a ghost. I reckon you startled me a bit; and in my business, surprises aren't usually good things."

My breathing had slowed enough for me to tell Thad about Jem's offer of the pack horse. Thad stepped closer to the fence and looked at the horses. "I reckon we could use a good pack horse," he said. "I know one of those hombres was riding the pinto because it had a saddle on it when we found their camp." Turning toward me, he asked, "Do you remember which of those bays is the pack horse?"

I smiled. "The one in the middle," I said.

"She looks good from here," he said. He turned toward Jem. "You've had a close look at her. What do you think?"

"She's about four years old and looks healthy," Jem said. "I'd keep her if I was you."

Thad nodded at me, and we gained a pack horse. We had made our first stock trade without even leaving the ranch, and no one near us knew about the deal. As I walked back to the house, I said, "Thank you, Lord! I reckon you really do work all things together for good for your children."

CHAPTER 8

The next morning Jem was smiling as he pushed his chair away from the table and stood. He and Thad had saddled the horses and loaded Jem's pack horse with supplies while I was cooking breakfast. I had given the rustlers their food just before the rest of us sat down to eat.

"Thank you for that fine breakfast, Miss Ruth," Jem said. He looked at Thad. "And thank you for the prayer you said before we ate. I'm a God-fearin' man, and I pray every day that God will guide me and protect me." He looked at Thad and me, then at Sarah, Bart, and Billy, who still sat at the table.

"I don't have any kinfolks left," he said, "but while I'm on the trail, I'll be praying for you the way I'd pray for my own family if I had one."

Billy shoved his chair away from the table, ran to Jem, and threw his arms around Jem's waist. "We'll be your family, Mr. Jem!" he said. Leaning back so he could see Jem's face without letting go of him, Billy said, "We'll pray for you every day until you come back."

Jem hugged Billy and said, "I'd be much obliged for your prayers." He had taken a step or two toward the door when Billy stopped him.

"You are coming back, aren't you, Mr. Jem?" Billy's eyes were wide, and his lower lip trembled.

Jem stepped back to Billy and crouched in front of him so that they looked into each other's eyes. He put his hands on Billy's shoulders and spoke softly. "You have my word, Pardner."

The sun had just risen when Thad and I followed Jem onto the porch. He shook Thad's hand and put his left hand on Thad's shoulder.

"You're young," he said, "but you're a man to ride the river with. Take care of your family. I should be back in two or three weeks to check on you and bring you your share of the reward money."

I hadn't planned to, but when Jem turned to say goodbye to me, I threw my arms around his neck and hugged him. "You be careful, Jem," I said.

He hugged me gently and then stepped back and removed his hat. He smiled.

"Yes, Ma'am, I will be," he said.

He put on his hat and walked to his horse. After he had checked his prisoners' shackles, he mounted and rode away, leading the four horses behind him.

Thad and I watched until the riders disappeared into the brush. I felt an emptiness inside me that I hadn't felt since Ma had died. I heard a sniffling sound behind me; and I turned to find Sarah, Bart, and Billy standing in the doorway. Sarah had her arm around Billy's shoulder, and he was crying. I walked to them, knelt in front of Billy, and took his face in my hands.

"He'll come back, Billy," I said.

"Do you really believe that?" Sarah asked.

I looked at her and thought about it. Then I looked at my brothers.

"I reckon I do," I said.

Thad, who had stepped behind me, offered his hand and helped me to my feet. Reading the question in my eyes, he said, "I reckon I do too." He turned and stepped off the porch. After he had taken a few steps, he stopped, looked at us over his shoulder, and grinned. "Since nobody else seems to be doing our chores," he said, "I also reckon we'd better get busy."

During the next two weeks, we got comfortable with our daily routine. Every few days after I had finished my work, I'd saddle one of our horses and ride to the top of a low butte not far from the ranch. I could watch our ranch house, stable, and corral from there the way someone riding past might watch it.

Except for the fact that Ma and Pa were missing, everything looked right from up there. My family looked like any other ranch family. Sarah washed our clothes and hung them on a line to dry. Billy fed the chickens and gathered eggs while Bart milked our cow. Sometimes both boys cleaned the stalls or disappeared with their fishing poles. Thad made repairs on both the house and the barn roofs, replaced broken or rotted rails and posts in the corral, and kept us supplied with meat by hunting. When he shot larger game like an elk or a mule deer, he dressed the carcass, quartered it, and either salted it or hung it in our smokehouse.

I had time to think and to pray while I watched our ranch. I thought a lot about Jem, and I sometimes wondered why Pa hadn't been like him. If he had, I reckoned all five of us would have missed Pa the same way we missed Ma.

One beautiful spring day, I had finished my chores and had ridden to the top of the butte. For nearly an hour, I had been watching the ranch, praying, and enjoying the peaceful feeling I always found up there.

As I took one last look before I started back to the ranch, I saw movement in the brush about a mile away to the east. Squinting and shielding my eyes with my hands, I could make out a rider leading a pack horse.

"Jem," I whispered. Turning in the saddle, I groped the contents of one of the saddlebags until I felt Pa's old brass telescope. Holding it to my eye, I scanned the landscape, trying to find the rider. "Please, God, let it be Jem," I said. When I finally located the blurry rider, my hands trembled as I focused the telescope.

I gasped and shoved the telescope back into the saddlebag. Trying to catch my breath, I dug my heels into the sides of my horse and started her down the butte. Jem wasn't riding toward our ranch, but Sheriff Tom Packard was.

The ride from the top of the butte to the ranch was usually pleasant and relaxing. That day it seemed twice as long, and my hands ached from gripping the reins so tightly. As I stopped the mare in front of the stable and dismounted, I breathed a sigh of relief. The sheriff's horses weren't visible. I had beaten him to the ranch.

I looped the reins around the hitching rail and ran to the house. Sarah sat in a chair, mending a hole in someone's sock. She gave me a worried look.

"What's wrong, Ruth?" she asked.

"Sheriff Packard's coming," I said. "Where's Billy?"

Sarah stood and laid the sock aside. "He and Bart went fishing," she said.

"Good!" I said. "We won't have to worry about them spilling the beans."

"What beans?" Sarah asked.

I had been walking toward the door, but I stopped and spun to look at Sarah. She was giggling.

"This is not the time, Sarah," I said.

She straightened her face. "You're right," she said. "I'm sorry." She started to giggle again but put her hand over her mouth.

"Where's Thad?" I asked.

"Right behind you," she said. Sarah started to giggle, but her eyes widened, and she stopped herself.

From behind me Thad asked, "Has either of you seen Pa this morning?"

A chill ran down my spine as I turned to face Thad. He stood a few steps inside the doorway, and Sheriff Packard stood behind him.

CHAPTER 9

"Howdy, Sheriff Packard," I said. I gave him one of my best smiles, but he ignored it.

"I'm here to talk to your pa," he said.

Now, I reckon if I named all the folks I don't like, I'd have a short list. But the first name on that list would be Tom Packard. He was mean, rude, foul-mouthed, and foul-smelling. Being pleasant toward him was always a chore, but I kept smiling.

"I haven't seen him this morning," I said. I looked at Sarah.

"I haven't either," she said.

"Last time I saw him," Thad said, "he was out near the fishing hole; but I doubt if you'd find him there now."

"Could we help you, Sheriff?" I asked. "Would you like a cup of coffee?"

He mumbled something, took off his hat, pulled out a chair, and sat at the table. When I placed a tin cup full of coffee in front of him, he nodded at me. I reckoned that was as close to saying thank you as he ever got. He took a sip and set the cup on the table.

When the sheriff spoke, he ignored me and talked to Thad. "I'm tracking a killer," he said, "and I want your pa to come with me. He's a better tracker than I am, and he can handle a rifle."

Thad glanced at me, and I nodded slightly.

"What can you tell us about this killer?" Thad asked. "If Pa doesn't return before you leave, we can pass along the information. If Pa can catch up with you, he will. We can watch for this killer around here too."

The sheriff drank the rest of his coffee and stood. "You stay as far away from him as you can," he said. "This cold-blooded hombre enjoys killing." He put on his hat. "His latest victims were headed west in their Conestoga wagon when he met them. The youngest daughter survived, and she told the folks who rescued her that the man seemed real friendly at first. After they fed him supper, he thanked them. Then he pulled his six-gun and shot her ma, her pa, and her two older brothers. He shot at her as she ran into the brush. She fell just as he shot, so his bullet only scratched her arm. He must have reckoned she'd die in the brush, so he didn't bother looking for her. He took their valuables and rode away. It was two days before anybody could get her to talk."

We looked at each other without speaking as the sheriff walked to the door and opened it. "Tell your pa I'm headed toward Tucson," he said. "I'll mark the trail if I turn to either side. He had started to close the door behind him when Thad spoke.

"Wait, Sheriff," he said. "You haven't told us what this man looks like."

"The little girl couldn't give a very good description," he said. "She said he was a tall black man who smoked a pipe." He closed the door and was gone.

Thad, Sarah, and I sat like stone statues at the table for what seemed like an hour although I reckoned it was really more like a few minutes. Thad stood, stepped behind his chair, and pushed it against the table.

"We all know Jem's not the killer," he said.

"You mean," I said, "we all *hope* Jem's not the killer." I leaned forward, rested my elbows on the table and my chin on my folded hands. I looked up at Thad. "We can't assume that Jem isn't the killer just because we like him," I said.

Sarah, seated to my right, turned to look at me, her eyes wide. She shook her head and sat up straight.

"We also can't assume Jem *is* the killer because he's tall, black, and smokes a pipe," she said.

"You're both right," Thad said. He leaned forward and put both hands flat on the table. Looking first into my eyes and then into Sarah's, he took a deep breath and let it out slowly. "I reckon if Jem is the kind of man that could shoot down a family like this killer did," he said, "he still could have ridden onto our place the way he did and fooled me into thinking about him the way I do." He turned and paced back and forth along the length of the table twice. Stopping in the middle of the table, Thad faced us again and shook his finger at us. "But" he said, "I don't reckon he could have fooled all three of us. Do you?"

I looked at Sarah, then at Thad. "You're right," I said. "Jem would never do something like that. I—"

The door banged open, and Bart and Billy stumbled into the kitchen. Between them they half-dragged, half-carried a stringer that held eight large catfish. Both boys were panting and sweating. Both were also grinning.

"We saw Sheriff Packard on his horse!" Billy said. "Did he—"

"Get those fish out of here!" I said.

Bart and Billy looked at the fish as if they'd forgotten they were holding the stringer. I reckon, in their excitement over seeing the sheriff on our property, they really had forgotten. Both of them looked surprised.

"We're sorry, Ruth," Bart said. He backed onto the porch, pulling the fish and Billy with him.

"Throw them on the cleaning table," Thad said. "Then come back. I'll help you clean them when we're finished talking."

Billy was wiping his sleeve across his eyes when he came back into the house. Between sobs, he said, "I'm real sorry Ruth. I know you don't want the house to smell like fish, but I had to tell you the sheriff was coming—"

"It's all right, Billy," I said. "They were only in here for a minute. I don't reckon that was long enough to make the house stink." I smiled. "You two I can smell from here. Let's talk outside so we won't have to wait for you to get cleaned up."

Sarah and I sat on the chairs, and the boys shared one of the benches. When Thad had finished telling Bart and Billy about our visit with the sheriff, he leaned forward with his elbows on his knees and looked at his brothers.

"Your turn," he said. "What did you see while you were fishing?"

"We seen the sheriff ride by, leading his pack horse," Billy said.

"Did you talk to him?" I asked. "Did he ask about Pa?"

Billy looked at Thad. "I thought you said it was our turn to talk," he said.

I held up my hands. "It is your turn, Billy," I said. "I'm sorry. I won't interrupt you again."

Billy grinned. "Bart and me didn't talk to the sheriff because he never saw us. We saw him first, so we laid flat on the ground behind some rocks until he was gone."

Thad and I both let out a sigh of relief. "Good work, Boys," he said. "That was a smart move."

"It sure was," I said, "but what if he had seen you and started asking questions?"

Bart and Billy looked at each other and then at me. "We'd have pretended we was dead!" Billy said.

I looked at Thad. He grinned and shrugged his shoulders. "I hadn't thought of that," he said.

Trying not to laugh, I stood and stepped in front of the boys. Bart watched me, but Billy closed his eyes.

"This is a good chance for us to practice," I said. "I'll be the sheriff. You're fishing." I took two steps back and spoke in my best sheriff's voice.

"Well, if it ain't the Martin boys," I said. "Are you catching anything?"

Bart grinned and held up his pretend stringer of catfish. Billy sat still and silent, his eyes closed.

"Billy," I said in my own voice. "What are you doing?"

When Billy didn't move, Bart leaned over and faced him. They were so close that their noses touched. Bart turned to face me and took off his hat.

"I'm sorry, Sheriff Ruth," he said, "but I reckon Billy's dead."

When we finally stopped laughing, I decided to try one more time. I explained that no one would be playing dead. The boys had to talk to the sheriff without giving away our secret.

"Well, if it ain't the Martin boys," I said. "Are you catching anything?"

Bart held up his pretend stringer again. He and Billy grinned at me.

"I'd like to talk to your pa," I said. "You boys know where he is?"

Bart focused on his pretend fishing pole. "Last time I saw him, he was near here," he said. "I don't reckon he's gone too far since then."

"Bart!" I said. "Pa's buried right there!"

Bart looked confused. "You couldn't know he is," he said. "Ain't you the sheriff?"

I looked at Thad. He shrugged his shoulders and grinned. "I reckon he's right, Ruth," he said.

I felt like screaming, but I was afraid the sheriff might still be close enough to hear me. I didn't want him coming back to the ranch to ask more questions.

"All right," I said, "no more pretending. We have work to do. Come with me, Sarah."

I had started to go back into the house when Billy said, "The other man didn't see us either."

"Billy," I said, "no more pretending!"

"He ain't pretending, Ruth," Bart said. "There was another man. He was following the sheriff, but I don't reckon the sheriff knew about him because the man was real quiet."

I felt a knot forming in my stomach. I took a deep breath and let it out slowly. I didn't want to worry my little brothers.

"What did he look like?" I asked.

Billy stared at me. "You know what the sheriff looks like," he said.

I gritted my teeth and reminded myself that Billy was only eight. "What did the other man look like?" I asked.

Bart and Billy looked at each other, then at me. Both of them shrugged.

"He was so quiet," Bart said, "that he had almost passed us before we knew he was there. We only saw him from the back."

I returned to my chair. "Tell me what he looked like from the back," I said.

Bart closed his eyes. "He wore a brown vest and a blue shirt, and I reckon his pants and his hat were black," he said.

73

"He was brown," Billy said. "From the back, he looked like Jem. His horse and his pack horse were brown too, but his bandana was red."

I looked at Thad. He jumped off the bench and started toward the stable. Over his shoulder, he said, "I'll saddle the horses. You grab our guns and a canteen."

"Ruth, where are you going?" Sarah asked.

I took off my apron and hung it over a chair. "You and the boys know what work you need to do," I said. "We need to save Sheriff Packard. We'll be back as soon as we can be."

CHAPTER 10

Thad and I rode toward the swimming hole at a gallop. We didn't slow our horses to a walk until we had passed it and ridden a good distance into the brush. I reckoned Thad was as scared as I was. We rode without talking for a while.

"What will we do when we catch up with them?" I asked.

"I've been thinking about that," Thad said. "We don't know what we'll find. Since we haven't heard any shooting, I reckon the hombre that's trailing Sheriff Packard hasn't made his move yet."

He stopped his horse and looked at me. "Ruth, I reckon Sheriff Packard is worth risking our necks for, even though we don't always agree with his way of doing things." He took off his hat and wiped his forehead with his sleeve. "We're going to run into the other man first, and he'll likely try to kill us." He put his hat on. "I don't know if I have inside me what it takes to shoot someone, even to save the sheriff's life."

The same thought had been troubling me. We had both killed animals; but shooting and possibly killing a man—however bad he was—would be a different matter. We started our horses at a trot. The sheriff had at least an hour's head start on us, but he and the man who trailed him were more than likely walking their horses. When Thad reckoned we were getting close, we slowed our horses to a walk too.

I had been praying as well as thinking while we rode, and something had occurred to me.

"Thad," I asked, "what kind of lawman do you reckon Sheriff Packard is?"

"Pa always said Sheriff Packard was a good one," Thad said. "Why?"

"The man trailing the sheriff has the edge right now because Sheriff Packard doesn't know he's there, right?" I asked.

"I reckon," Thad said.

"What if we could let the sheriff know he's being followed?" I asked.

"In an even fight with most outlaws," Thad said, "I wouldn't worry about Sheriff Packard. But how can we warn him without getting ourselves shot?"

I told him my idea, and he liked it. Again, we rode forward, watching and listening. A light breeze blew against our faces. Neither of us saw or heard anything, but we both smelled the pipe.

After tying our horses to a palo verde tree, we moved forward on foot. Thad quietly worked the lever to feed a cartridge into the rifle's empty chamber. Both barrels of my shotgun were loaded.

Using rocks and brush for cover, we crept forward. Flies buzzed around my head. Sweat dripped from my chin, but I shivered from the cold inside me. We stopped every few yards to watch and listen. I had just started to move from behind a creosote bush when Thad stopped me with a hand on my shoulder. He pointed to our right, and I saw the two horses.

After watching long enough to make sure nobody was with the horses, we started forward again. For the next fifty or sixty yards, nothing looked out of place. I reckon we wouldn't have spotted the man if he hadn't moved, but he stood up. As he lifted his rifle to his shoulder, Thad and I hit the ground on our backs. I pulled the hammers on the shotgun back and fired one barrel into the air, then the second barrel. At the same time, Thad fired his rifle into the air twice.

With my ears ringing, I broke open the shotgun, ejected the spent shells, and shoved them into my pocket. From my other pocket, I dug out two fresh shells, thumbed them into the chambers, and snapped the shotgun closed. I glanced at Thad in time to see him work the lever on his rifle, ejecting an empty cartridge and sliding a fresh one into place. He grinned at me as he picked up the empty brass shells and dropped them into one of his vest pockets.

"Good plan, Ruth," he said. "I reckon we got Sheriff Packard's attention."

Both of us were propped on our elbows, but we flattened against the ground again as several shots sounded and bullets whizzed over our heads, clipping the bushes.

With my head resting on the ground, facing Thad, I said, "I reckon we got someone else's attention too."

We stayed put for the next half hour or so, listening to gunfire. No more bullets came our way, so we felt safe enough to raise our heads to drink from the canteen we'd brought along. Lying there in the sun, I wondered if I was feeling what a chicken felt when I roasted it.

What seemed like a long time after the shooting had stopped, we heard someone moving through the brush. I prayed that Sheriff Packard was making the noise; but when I raised up far enough to see, I didn't recognize the man coming toward us. He was limping, and his red bandana was tied around the upper part of his right arm. I reckoned he was headed toward his horses, walking in a direction that would take him far enough away from our hiding place that he wouldn't see us. I didn't realize that I'd been holding my breath. I started to let it out, relieved by what I'd seen. Then I gasped when I thought about what I *hadn't* seen. Where was Sheriff Packard? The outlaw had been wounded. Had he wounded the sheriff too? Worse yet, had he killed the sheriff? I felt sick.

Thad was lying on his stomach. Using both hands, he raised himself off the ground and stretched his neck until he could see the outlaw. When he lowered himself, he was grinning at me. I reckon he must have read my thoughts from the look on my face. Still grinning, he motioned for me to take another look. The outlaw still limped toward his horse, but Sheriff Packard followed ten feet behind him. He led his own horse and his pack horse, holding the reins in his left hand. His right hand held his six-gun, and he was pointing it at the outlaw.

"Thank you, Lord," I whispered. I looked at Thad. "Let's make sure Sheriff Packard is all right."

I started to stand and call out to the sheriff, but Thad grabbed my arm and pulled me back down. He put a finger to his lips and leaned closer to me.

"I reckon the sheriff might get a little excited if we jump out from behind this bush and holler at him," Thad whispered. "He might mistake us for that hombre's pardners and shoot us."

Thad was right. I didn't want Sheriff Packard to shoot me. At the same time, I didn't much care for the thought of lying there on the ground while the sun broiled me either.

"What are we going to do?" I whispered.

"Wait," Thad said.

We waited while the sheriff shackled the outlaw's hands behind his back. We waited while the sheriff failed twice to help the outlaw mount his horse. He succeeded on the third attempt, drank from his canteen, checked his saddle girth, and then mounted his own horse. I jumped when Thad spoke.

"Sheriff Packard, Ruth and Thad Martin over here," he said.

I knew Sheriff Packard had drawn his six-gun as soon as Thad had spoken the first word. I knew he was aiming his gun toward us, and I knew he had thumbed the hammer back.

"Show yourselves, hands in the air," he said.

Thad and I stood beside each other, facing the sheriff and his prisoner.

"Are you alone?" he asked. His gun was still aimed in our general direction.

"Yes, Sir," Thad said.

"Are you armed?" he asked.

"Yes, Sir," Thad replied. "A rifle and a shotgun are lying on the ground in front of us."

"Where are your horses?" he asked.

"In the brush over yonder, Sir," Thad said.

Sheriff Packard shook his head. He pointed his gun toward the sky and lowered its hammer. He shook his head again and muttered a curse as he dropped the gun into its holster. When he spoke again, he sounded more irritated than angry.

"Put your hands down, pick up your weapons, and get your horses," he said. "On the ride between here and your ranch, you can explain to me what you two are doing out here, hiding in the brush." Still shaking his head, he took a deep breath and blew it out slowly. "You'd better have a mighty good reason, or I might lock you in my jail with this hombre."

CHAPTER 11

As we rode at a walk toward the Box M, the outlaw, who really did resemble Jem slightly, led the way so the sheriff could watch him. Thad and I, riding beside Sheriff Packard, told him what had happened after he left the ranch. He made no comment until several minutes after we had finished our story.

Turning to look at us, he raised his eyebrows. "I'm obliged to both of you," he said. "I reckon you saved my life." He frowned. "What you did was brave. It was also dangerous. Why would your pa let you do a fool thing like this instead of coming himself, or at least riding along with you?"

When I looked at Thad, he shook his head slightly. The question had surprised me too, but I reckoned Thad saw me as our best hope for a reasonable explanation on short notice.

"Pa wasn't around when Billy and Bart told us they'd seen this hombre following you," I said. "Thad and I reckoned waiting for Pa could have made us too late to warn you."

The outlaw muttered a few curses and glared at Thad and me over his shoulder. Sheriff Packard moved his horse ahead until it walked beside the outlaw's horse. Leaning toward the outlaw, he spoke quietly.

"You talk like that in front of this young lady again," he said, "I'll put a gag in your mouth until I get you to Tucson and lock you up."

He stopped his horse and waited until Thad and I had caught up with him. I thanked him for warning the outlaw. We rode in silence for a few minutes.

"I reckon you were right about not waiting for your pa," he said. "If you'd come along a few minutes later, we probably wouldn't be having this conversation." He had been looking ahead, watching the outlaw's back. He drank from his canteen and wiped sleeve across his mouth. Then he looked at Thad and me. "Your pa can get cantankerous at times," he said. "If you think he'll be angry with the two of you for riding off the way you did without telling him, I can have a word with him and maybe settle him down a bit."

"We're obliged, Sheriff Packard," Thad said, "but I don't reckon you'll need to do that. Pa has been a lot easier to get along with for the last few months."

"That's good news," the sheriff said.

We talked about a variety of things as we rode along—nothing serious, just passing the time. Sheriff Packard was almost pleasant. When we came to the place where Thad and I had to turn off the main trail to ride toward the ranch, the sheriff thanked us again for our help. We said goodbye and started our horses forward again.

"I'm thankful we don't have to do that every day," I said.

"So am I," Thad said, "but I reckon we handled things pretty well. Sheriff Packard doesn't suspect anything."

"Thank God that Billy and Bart weren't with us," I said. "I'm not sure they're ready to be around folks yet."

"They were right about that killer looking like Jem," Thad said, "at least, from the back."

As we rode from behind a butte that hid the ranch from us, Thad was ahead of me. He stopped so suddenly that my horse bumped his.

"I sure hope you're wrong about Bart and Billy being ready to be around other folks," he said, "because we have company."

When I stopped my horse next to Thad's, what I saw made me shudder. A large blue wagon with red wheels and a white canvas top sat in front of the stable. Besides Bart and Billy, I counted five children, a man, and a woman. The man was leading an ox into our corral to join a second ox and a horse I didn't recognize. The woman, holding a small child, was talking to Bart and Billy. I didn't see Sarah.

"Lord, please protect us," I said.

"Amen," Thad said. "As much as I want to let these horses run, I reckon those folks would get suspicious if we galloped in there with no good reason."

"Maybe the boys will see us coming and remember to mind their tongues," I said. Looking down at my hands, I realized that I was holding the reins in clinched fists. I took a deep breath and tried to relax. When I looked at Thad, he was shaking his head slowly.

"The young'uns must have invited those folks to stay the night," he said. "I reckon they've been here a while since that man is moving the last of his stock into our corral."

"And I reckon the boys have been talking to his wife the whole time he's been tending to the animals," I said.

"I don't see Sarah anywhere. I hope we're not riding into a mess."

"Have a little faith, Ruth," Thad said. "Maybe our little brothers will surprise us—and I don't reckon Sarah has run off."

When Thad and I stepped down from our horses and tied the reins to the hitching rail near the stable, Bart and Billy were already beside us. Both were talking, and I had to laugh.

"Whoa, Boys," I said. "Let's try this one at a time. Bart, you're the oldest; you talk first."

Bart looked at Billy, who had started to cry. "I'll let Billy talk first," he said.

I slid my arm around Bart's shoulders and hugged him. "Thank you, Bart," I said. "That was kind of you."

Billy, grinning now, wiped his sleeve across his eyes. He grabbed my hand and led me to where the woman stood, talking to her children. When she saw us coming, she stopped talking and smiled at me.

"You must be Ruth," she said. "I'm Kate Wells. My husband is Paul; and these are my children: John, David, Timothy, Edward, and—" she turned so that I could see the face of the child she held. "Rose."

Billy was still holding my hand. "They're going to California in their wagon," he said, "but they need to rest their oxes."

Sarah came out of the house just then. "Come and get it," she said. She looked happy—more like relieved—to see me. Something was wrong.

"You go ahead, Mrs. Wells," I said. "I'll be along in a minute."

I walked to the corral, where Thad and Mr. Wells stood, talking. Thad introduced us, and I told Mr. Wells that Sarah had prepared a meal. Thad and I watched him walk toward the house. He stopped at the wash basin on the porch, scrubbed his hands, and dried them on the towel that hung there. I waited for him to go inside before I spoke.

"What do you think about him?" I asked.

"I just met him," Thad said. "I don't reckon I've had enough time to think anything about him." He had been leaning against the corral fence, but he stood up straight and cocked his head a little to one side. "Why are you asking? We've had folks stop to rest for a day or two before. Did Mrs. Wells say something wrong?"

"She was friendly," I said, "but something doesn't feel right. Let's eat, and then we can talk to Sarah. I reckon it could just be my imagination."

Thad and I were a few steps away from the porch when the door opened. Bart and Billy walked onto the porch and closed the door behind them. Each boy carried a plate in one hand and a tin cup in the other. Billy was grinning, but Bart looked a little confused.

"What are you doing?" I asked.

Billy grinned. "We get to eat out here!" he said. He walked to the bench and sat down, putting his cup beside him. Bart started to follow him, but Thad stopped him.

"Hold on," Thad said. "Why aren't you eating at the table?"

Bart shrugged his shoulders. There ain't room," he said. "The Wells family took all the chairs." He walked to the bench and sat beside Billy.

I headed for the door, but Thad stepped in front of me. He held out both hands with his palms toward me.

"Easy, Ruth," he said. "Remember, these folks are company, and they'll just be here for a day or two. At least Sarah is eating at the table with them."

I closed my eyes and took two deep breaths, letting them out slowly. Thad grinned when I stepped back. Glancing at the boys, I realized that the only food on each plate was a thick slice of bread.

"Bart," I said, "is Sarah only feeding the Wells family bread?"

Bart finished chewing, took a drink from his cup, and frowned at me. "No," he said. "They get to eat chicken stew. Mr. Wells killed and plucked one of our chickens as soon as they got here. Mrs. Wells told Sarah to make a stew."

"Hold on a minute," I said. "Did Mr. Wells ask anybody if he could kill one of our chickens?"

"No," Bart said.

"Well," I said, "if Sarah made chicken stew, why aren't you and Billy eating it?"

Bart swallowed another chunk of bread, took another drink, and belched. He grinned at me. "I feel better!" he said. Seeing the look on my face, he stopped grinning. He looked at Thad. "We ain't at the table!" he said.

"You'd better answer her," Thad said.

"Mrs. Wells said there was only enough stew for their family," Bart said. He looked at Thad. "And Sarah ain't sitting at the table with the Wells family. Mrs. Wells kept her there to serve them their food."

This time when I headed for the door, Thad didn't try to stop me. Instead, he opened the door for me and stepped aside.

CHAPTER 12

I was already angry when I stepped into the house. When I saw what was happening around the table, I got plumb mad.

Three of the four boys were using their spoons like catapults, shooting chunks of chicken and vegetables at Sarah, who was using a plate as a shield. Judging by the amount of chicken scattered across the floor, either the boys were bad shots or Sarah had protected herself well with her shield. The fourth boy had laid his catapult on the table and was attempting—not very successfully—to spit chunks of stew into a tin cup he had placed in the middle of the table. Rose sat in the chair next to her mother's chair, slowly pouring the milk from her cup onto the floor.

Mr. and Mrs. Wells sat with their heads together, discussing something that I reckoned must have been more important than keeping their children from destroying our kitchen. Sarah was the first person to notice me, and she was distracted just long enough for a chunk of chicken to hit her right cheek.

Now, in spite of Pa's failures, he and Ma had raised all of us Martin children to respect our elders. I reckon that was the only reason Mr. and Mrs. Wells still sat at the table a few minutes later. Sarah and I had chased all five of the little Wells people out of the house. The oldest boy had carried his sister. I closed the door behind them and turned to face their parents.

Mr. and Mrs. Wells still sat at the table, but they had stopped talking about whatever was so important to them. Instead, they stared at Sarah and me. Mrs. Wells spoke first.

"Well, I never—"

"No, Ma'am," I said, "but I reckon if you had, those little piglets would be trained well enough to eat in the house."

Sarah had walked over to stand beside me. I heard her gasp; but when I looked at her, she grinned. I turned back to the Wells couple. "You folks came to us in need of rest, and we welcomed you. Your behavior has been poor, and we can't allow it to continue."

Mrs. Wells started to speak again, but I hadn't finished. "Your family and your livestock will have had a full day's rest by noon tomorrow when you leave. For now, I'd be obliged if you'd step outside and make some attempt to control your children. I reckon sending the oldest two back in here to help us clean up their mess would be a good start."

I hadn't given any thought to how Mr. and Mrs. Wells would respond to my words. They were sitting in our house on our land. I didn't expect them to be happy about leaving, but I wasn't giving them a choice. I was surprised when they looked at each other and smiled. When they turned toward Sarah and me, they were still smiling. This time Mr. Wells spoke.

"Katie and I are willing to forgive your rudeness to our children this one time because you're so young," he said. "In spite of your poor behavior, we like this place. We've decided to stay for a spell. There's plenty of food, and the house will suit us—your family should be comfortable in the barn for the next few months."

I couldn't believe what he was saying. I started for the parlor to get my shotgun. I stopped when Mrs. Wells spoke to her husband.

"You're right, Paul," she said. "Ruth is so young to be making important decisions. We should speak with her father."

I felt sick. I walked back to stand beside Sarah. I didn't know if Bart and Billy had let the truth about Pa slip out. And then I did.

Mr. Wells smiled at his wife. "I don't know, Dear," he said. "What if her father gets upset with us like she did? We wouldn't want him to get the sheriff involved, would we?"

They were still smiling as they turned to look at me. Even though I felt sick, I was mad clear through.

"You're crazy if you think we're going to work our ranch with you!" I said. Sarah had grabbed my hand, and she was squeezing it hard.

Mrs. Wells laughed. "We don't plan to work your ranch with you," she said. "We're here to rest, remember? Don't worry though; we'll stay out of your way while you work it. You can keep doing what you've been doing, and we'll guide you in your work."

"Think of us as your temporary parents," Mr. Wells said, "just filling in until your Pa returns."

I was trembling, and I thought I might throw up. "You won't get away with this," I said. We crossed the room, and Sarah had just started to close the door behind us when Mrs. Wells, still smiling, spoke.

"Come back in a few hours to get some of your things to take to the barn," she said. "Paul and I will separate the things you can take from the things we'll keep for our own use."

Sarah and I stepped off the porch and started toward the stable. The Wells children, who had been sitting on one bench and both chairs, stared at us silently until we had covered about half the distance. When we heard the door close, Sarah and I stopped to look back toward the house. The porch was empty.

"What are we going to do?" Sarah asked. She started to cry. I put my arm around her shoulder as we continued walking.

"I reckon we need to find the boys first," I said. "Then we need to talk, and we need to pray." I pulled Sarah closer and kissed her cheek. "If God rescued Jonah from the belly of that big fish, the three Hebrews from the fiery furnace, and Daniel from the lions' den, I just can't see Him having much of a problem saving us from the Wells family. Can you?"

The sound of someone hammering led us around behind the stable. Thad was nailing a loose board in place. I told him we needed to talk and asked him if he knew where the boys were.

"I sent them to fish," Thad said. "I reckoned we'd need some extra food, and I was hoping to keep Mr. Wells from killing another chicken." He grinned. "Do you want me to fetch the boys?"

"No," I said. "Let's go to the swimming hole. We need some privacy. Are you finished here?"

"Yes," he said. "Ruth, what's wrong?" His grin had disappeared.

As we walked toward the swimming hole, I told Thad what had happened. While he listened, he kept tossing the hammer into the air, making it spin, and catching it by its handle. By the time I had finished, we were close enough to see the boys.

"How much are we going to tell our fishermen?" Thad asked.

"I reckon we should tell them everything," I said. "They're old enough to hear it, and one—or both of them got us into this mess." I brushed a fly away from my face. "Besides, we may need their help if we're going to get rid of the Wells family."

"Oh," Thad said. He tossed the hammer high enough into the air that it flipped twice before he caught it by the handle. "We *are* going to get rid of them. Let's talk to the young'uns."

I wasn't even a little surprised when Billy started sobbing. Since we couldn't understand what he was saying, we turned to Bart.

"Mrs. Wells tricked us," Bart said. "Billy and me was playing with her kids, and she asked about our parents. You never said we couldn't tell folks about Ma, so we told her." Bart still had his line in the water, and he kept an eye on his cork. "She looked really sad, and she said she was sorry for our loss. When she asked about Pa, we told her he was away today."

"You did well, Bart," I said. Billy sat with his face buried in his hands, still crying. "And so did you, Billy."

Without moving, Billy said into his hands, "No, I didn't! He ain't done yet."

"What happened next?" I asked.

"Mrs. Wells didn't say anything else for a spell," Bart said, "and we were playing with her kids." He grabbed his pole and gave it a jerk. "Got one!" he said.

Thad, Sarah, and I waited while he added a catfish to their stringer, baited his hook, and tossed the line back into the water. "Watch your cork, Billy," he said. "Something's playing with your bait."

Bart looked at us. "Where was I?" he asked.

"You were playing with the Wells kids," Sarah said, "and Mrs. Wells hadn't said anything."

"But then she did," Bart said. "We was playing marbles; and she asks, in kind of a sad voice, how long Pa's been gone. She'd been so kind to us that I reckon we'd both let our guard down. Billy was the one that told her Pa had passed in January, but I was getting ready to say the same thing."

"She did trick you for certain," Thad said. "I reckon the Devil himself couldn't have done a better job."

Billy sat up and looked at us. "I'm sorry," he said.

"It wasn't your fault, Billy," Thad said. "Hey! Your cork just went under! We'll talk about making things right after you land that fish."

Something like an hour later, the five of us were still sitting on the ground at the edge of the swimming hole. While the boys had continued to catch fish, we had looked for some way to get rid of the Wells family. We had come up with nothing.

"Maybe Jem can help us," Billy said.

"Well, maybe he could, Billy," I said. I gritted my teeth. I didn't want to make Billy cry again. "But then, Jem isn't here, is he?"

Billy grinned and pointed over my shoulder. None of us had heard or seen him coming, but there stood Jem, not more than fifty feet away. He held his broad-brimmed hat in one hand and the reins of his horses in the other. He smiled at us.

"Why do you young'uns look so surprised?" he asked. "I told y'all I'd be back."

CHAPTER 13

I don't reckon I have the right words to describe what I felt when I saw Jem standing there. I had been ready to give up; but, seeing him gave me hope. Sarah and I ran to him and hugged him. He shook hands with Thad and Bart, hugged Billy, and then walked to the swimming hole and sat with us.

"I rode past your ranch house on the way here," he said, "and noticed you have some company. I'd be happy to hear what's happened since I left—that is, if you want to tell me. Before you start, though, I have a favor to ask of y'all. I'm real hungry, and I see fish on your stringer. If I could build a fire, get my frying pan from the pack horse, and clean a couple of those fish, I could cook and eat them while you're talking." He stood, put on his hat, and moved silently toward his horses. He had covered half the distance when he stopped, looked at us over his shoulder, and smiled. "I hate to waste a good cook fire," he said. "I reckon I'll boil some coffee too."

While Jem sat cross-legged, facing us, eating fish, and drinking coffee, Thad and I told him about the Wells family. He listened without comment until we had finished. After he had swallowed his last bite of fish, he filled his cup from the coffee pot and took a drink.

We sat in silence, watching him. Jem continued to sip his coffee while he studied our faces over the rim of his cup.

"I reckon those Wells folks have sure enough put you between a rock and a hard place," he said. He pushed his hat back and rubbed his forehead. "The way I see it, you have two choices. You can either move into the stable until the Wells family leaves—"

"No!" I said. "Those squatters aren't going to take our house away from us!"

"She's right, Jem," Thad said.

"All right," Jem said. "Unless I'm missing something, your other option is to disarm them." Jem poured the last of the coffee into his cup and set the pot on the ground.

"What do you mean?" I asked.

"Why don't you go back to the house right now and make them leave?" Jem asked.

"If we do," Sarah said, "they'll tell Sheriff Packard that Pa's dead, and the sheriff will take us to—"

I tried to stop Sarah, but I was too late. Billy wailed, "We're going to the orphan house!"

It took us a good while to get Billy settled down; but when we finally did, we picked up our conversation where Sarah had left off.

"Mr. and Mrs. Wells will tell on us," I said. "That's their weapon. How can we disarm them?"

"I haven't figured that out yet," Jem said, "but there has to be a way. You're sure about what will happen if—" Jem looked at Billy, who was pretending to shoot at a buzzard that circled above us.

"Yes," I said. "He may not be a good person; but he's a good lawman, who feels bound to uphold the law. Too bad we don't have a sheriff who's a little more—"

"Wait a minute!" Thad said. All of us—except Jem—jumped when Thad slapped his thigh. His eyes were wide, and so was his grin. "You were right, Ruth," he said.

"About what?" I asked.

"Remember the day you found Pa in the stable?"

I nodded. "What about it?" I asked.

"You told us Pa didn't have to be alive for us to stay on our ranch. You said we just had to make people *think* Pa was alive."

My heart sank. "Thad, Mr. and Mrs. Wells already know Pa's dead," I said. "It's too late—"

"I know," he said. He waved his hand and shook his head. He was getting more excited. "But they don't know Sheriff Packard!"

I looked from Sarah to Jem, but they were as confused as I was. "I'm sorry, Thad," I said, "but you're not making sense."

"Yes, I am," he said. "Think about it. Jem was right. We need to disarm Mr. and Mrs. Wells, but we don't need to tell the sheriff Pa's dead. We just need to make them *think* we're telling the sheriff!"

"I reckon one of us must be loco, Thad," I said.

"Maybe not, Ruth," Jem said. "I reckon I know where he's headed. Let him talk."

"If Mr. and Mrs. Wells see us tell the sheriff about Pa," Thad said, "and he says we can stay on the ranch by ourselves, we'll have disarmed them! They'll pack up and move on."

I laughed. "You know Sheriff Packard will never let us stay at the ranch on our own," I said.

Thad grinned and raised his eyebrows. "Who said anything about Sheriff Packard?"

I looked at Jem; and, smiling, he touched the brim of his hat with two fingers. "Sheriff Jem at your service, Ma'am."

I shook my head. "You can't be serious," I said. "We'd never get away with something that crazy!"

"Do you have a better idea?" Thad asked.

"Nobody said it would be easy," Jem said, "but I reckon it's possible."

"You can't be a sheriff, Jem," I said. I was still shaking my head. "You're—" I stopped. I could feel my cheeks turning red.

"You're black!" Billy said.

Jem's eyes widened, and his mouth opened as he looked at his hands. "I *am* black!" he said. Then he laughed. "Ruth," he said, "some of my former fellow buffalo soldiers came out west after the war like me. They've been fighting Indians and protecting settlements ever since. This Wells family ain't from around here. They don't know how we do things out here. If we play this right, I reckon we can run them off your ranch and send them on their way before they know what hit them."

Billy jumped up and started punching at an imaginary enemy. "You can hit Mr. and Mrs. Wells," he said. "Bart and me will hit them kids before they know it!"

Thad grinned at me. "Maybe," he said, "we should have Bart and Billy catch some more fish while we make our plans."

Once the boys had started fishing again, the rest of us moved farther away from them so we could talk. We had to make sure that Mr. and Mrs. Wells believed what they saw and heard. An hour later, we reckoned our plan was near perfect. Then Sarah found a flaw.

"Wait," she said. "What about the boys? They're going to want to have a part in this too."

"I reckon we could send them down here to fish," Thad said.

"I'd feel safer if they were close enough for us to keep an eye on them," I said.

"You're right," Thad said. "They'll want to help too."

"We'll just have to make sure they understand how important it is they play their roles," I said. "Let's bring them over here and talk to them."

Bart and Billy sat facing me while I explained what we wanted them to do and told them why. When I had finished, I asked, "Do you have any questions?"

Billy raised his hand. "Yes, Billy," I said.

His little forehead wrinkled as he squinted at me. "So, now we don't get to hit them, right?"

CHAPTER 14

I knew that the Bible teaches us not to hate people, and I had never been a hateful person. Still, when Jem rode into the brush, and the five of us started walking toward the house, I found myself having to work really hard at not hating Mr. and Mrs. Wells. While they slept in our beds that night, we would be lying on our bedrolls in the stable. If our plan worked, we'd only spend one night there; but I still struggled with our situation.

When we got close to the house, I stopped. "Remember," I said, "the Wells family has taken over our home. They'll expect us to be sad and angry. We can't let them know about our plan. They need to believe they're in charge." I looked at Bart and Billy. "If something happens and you don't know what to say, don't say anything. Let Thad, Sarah, and me do the talking." I smiled at them. "This won't be easy, but God is on our side. Now, let's go fool the Wells family."

"Where have you been?" Mrs. Wells asked. She stood on the porch with her hands on her hips, staring at us.

"Fishing," Thad said. Sarah and I stepped aside, and he pointed to Bart and Billy, who held the heavy stringer between them. He helped them lift the fish onto the cleaning table, and then spoke without looking at Mrs. Wells. "We'll clean these so we can cook them for supper."

Mrs. Wells hadn't moved. "All of you didn't need to go," she said. "Who did you think was going to do the work that needs to be done here?"

Before anyone else could respond, Billy stepped forward and said, "We reckoned you and your children might do it."

Her face was twisted with anger as she stepped off the porch toward Billy. When she raised her hand to strike him, Thad stepped in front of her. He spoke quietly but firmly.

"Ma'am, you may do a lot of things in your lifetime, but you'll never strike one of us."

Just before she turned and stomped into the house, I was sure I saw fear in her eyes. When the door had slammed behind her, four of us turned to look at Billy.

"What happened," I asked, "to not saying anything if you didn't know what to say?"

Billy looked confused. "I *did* know what to say, so I said it."

I looked at Thad and Sarah. Both of them were grinning. Thad shrugged his shoulders.

"I reckon he did," he said.

While Sarah and I cooked the fish and boiled some yucca root, the boys did some of their chores. As we worked, the Wells family sat in *our* parlor, reading *our* books. The younger children played with *our* toys while they waited to eat *our* food. When I told them the meal was ready, I didn't have to pretend I didn't like them.

After they had finished their meal, the whole family went outside. While Mr. and Mrs. Wells sat in the chairs on the porch, the children played.

Sarah and I washed and dried the dishes. I set them back on the table while Sarah fetched the boys. After they had washed up, we ate what the Wells family had left us. When the food was gone, the boys thanked us and went to the stable to lay out our bedrolls. Sarah and I washed the dishes, pans, and eating utensils again. Then we swept the floor and headed for the stable, walking past the Wells family without speaking.

We sat in a circle inside one of the stalls. The straw under our bedrolls smelled good and made us comfortable. I tried to hide my anger when I spoke.

"I reckon we've done all we can for today," I said.

"Shouldn't we pray?" Bart asked.

"We should," I said. "I just didn't get that far yet." I reached for Billy's hand on one side of me and Sarah's on the other. The boys joined hands, and I looked at Bart. "Will you please pray?" I asked.

When Bart finished his prayer, we sat in silence. There was still enough light coming through the stable door for me to see the rifle leaning against the wall in one corner of the stall and the shotgun in the other. Thad had handed the weapons and extra cartridges out one of the parlor windows while the Wells family sat on the porch. Bart and Billy had hidden both guns and cartridges in the wheelbarrow under some hay and then moved them to the stable. Since we hadn't known how Mr. and Mrs. Wells would feel about our keeping our guns, we reckoned we'd just take them without asking.

"I reckon we've fooled the Wells family so far," I said, "but we're not out of the woods yet. We—"

"When were we in the woods?" Billy asked.

111

"She means we're not out of danger yet, Billy," Sarah said.

Billy gave me a confused look. "Why didn't you just say that?" he asked.

"I'm sorry, Billy," I said. "We're not out of danger yet. We still have to get through breakfast and part of the morning tomorrow." I looked at Bart and Billy.

"When Jem gets here tomorrow—"

"You mean *Sheriff* Jem?" Billy asked.

I took a deep breath and let it out slowly. "Yes," I said. "Sheriff Jem. When he gets here tomorrow, the Wells family needs to think we're as surprised to see him as they are." I looked at Thad.

"When he tells us he knows Pa is dead," Thad said, "remember what we're supposed to do. Let's get some sleep. We can talk more in the morning."

I lay awake long after the others had gone to sleep— partly because I was still angry with the Wells family and partly because I was worried about whether or not our plan would work. I prayed, asking God to lead and protect us. At some point during my talk with Him, I fell asleep. I awoke to the crowing of a rooster.

Before we left the stall, we joined hands again and asked God for His help. When I had finished praying, I looked at the four people I loved most. "We can do this," I said.

Bart grinned at me. "We can do all things through Christ, who strengthens us!' he said.

I hugged him. "I reckon we can," I said.

"And," Billy said "we're the Box M Gang!"

"I reckon we are," Thad said. "All of us need to remember this is a day just like any other day. We'll just go about our business and see what happens."

As Sarah and I started toward the house, the boys separated to do their chores. Sarah took my hand and smiled. "Welcome," she said, "to the first performance of the Martin Family Players." She was still smiling when we stepped onto the porch. Bowing slightly, she said, "Act One, Scene One," and opened the door.

The house was quiet for a while, but the Wells family finally dragged themselves out of *our* beds, prepared for the day, and gathered at *our* table. They didn't speak to us.

Sarah and I had a tall stack of flapjacks and a pitcher of milk waiting for them. They spoke to each other while they ate, but they continued to ignore us. We were grateful to be left alone.

When they had finished, they left the table without saying "thank you"—not even a grunt of gratitude—and disappeared into the parlor. Sarah and I smiled at the thought of this being the last meal we would have to prepare for them.

I cooked more flapjacks while Sarah rounded up the boys. Because the Wells family sat in the next room, we only talked about unimportant things. Any serious talking would need to be done outside.

When we had finished eating, the boys returned to their chores. Sarah and I were putting away the last of the dishes when I heard something behind me. I turned in time to see the oldest Wells boy walking into the parlor. He had left a large basket of soiled clothes on the table.

I was struggling to control my anger, but when I glanced at Sarah, I burst out laughing. She held a box of wooden matches in one hand and a coal-oil lamp in the other. Grinning at me, she nodded her head toward the basket and whispered, "It's my turn to do laundry!"

As soon as she set the lamp and the matches on a table, I grabbed her hand and dragged her across the room. We didn't stop until we had closed the door behind us and stepped off the porch. Then we let loose and laughed till we cried.

CHAPTER 15

The temptation to follow Sarah's idea for what to do with the Wells family's clothes was strong, but we reckoned washing them was a better plan. Still, we washed our clothes first.

Pa had dug a well about halfway between the house and the stable. To make Ma's work as easy as possible, he had put her wash tubs, made from cutting a large wooden barrel in half, about twenty feet from the well. He had also set two posts about thirty feet apart. Each post was about six feet tall with a cross piece, about four feet long, fastened to the top. Ma had run a piece of thin rope between the ends of the cross pieces to make her clotheslines. Then she had Pa notch one end of two poles about seven feet long, and she used those to support the sagging lines halfway between the posts.

Sarah and I filled metal buckets from the well and emptied three into each tub. Kneeling beside one of the tubs, I pulled a dirty shirt from our basket and plunged it into the water. I scrubbed it with a bar of lye soap, wrung it out, and handed it to Sarah, who was kneeling beside the other tub. She rinsed as much of the soap from the shirt as she could and wrung it out again. Then she stood, carried the shirt to the clothesline, and fastened it to the line with two wooden clothespins.

I had just dropped a second shirt into Sarah's tub when she returned. She rinsed the shirt and was wringing it out when she spoke.

"You know, Ruth Martin," she said, "if we take our time on our laundry, we might not get to Mrs. Wells's basket before Sheriff Jem gets here."

"I reckon you're right, Sarah Martin," I said. "We'd best slow down a bit. In fact, I've been thinking. We didn't boil the laundry or soak it overnight because nothing was filthy. Maybe we were wrong." I grabbed the shirt she was holding and dropped into my soapy water. "I'm going to make sure this shirt is really clean."

I don't recall ever laughing as much over laundry as we did that morning. The Wells children came outside and played, chasing each other, hiding, laughing, and screaming. Mr. and Mrs. Wells stayed inside the house.

An hour or so later, I saw Billy running toward us. His hat, bouncing behind his head on its stampede string, looked like some strange creature chasing him. I stood and handed Sarah a pair of pants I had just wrung out.

"I don't see Bart," Sarah said, "but Billy sure is in a hurry. Maybe they caught something really big."

"No," I said, "Billy would be hollering if they had. Something's wrong."

When Billy stopped in front of me, I knelt and put both hands on his shoulders. "Catch your breath," I said. "Is Bart all right?"

Billy nodded. "The sheriff—" he said.

"Easy, Billy," I said. "Take your time."

"Me and Bart was fishing," he said, "and we seen— we saw the sheriff riding toward the ranch."

I smiled. "He may be a mite early," I said, "but we're ready for him. Go get Bart and then come back here so you two can help us get those—"

"No!" Billy shook my hands from his shoulders and stepped forward, so his face was only a few inches from mine. "We saw Sheriff Packard!"

It took me a minute to understand what Billy had just told me. I reckoned I had misunderstood what he said.

"Are you sure you saw Sheriff Packard?" I asked.

"Yep," Billy said.

"Did you talk to him?" I asked.

"Nope," Billy said, "he was too far away." Reaching over his shoulder, he grabbed his hat and shoved it onto his head. "He wasn't riding fast, so I reckon he's not quite to the swimming hole yet. Bart told me to run here and tell you. What are we going to do?"

I felt sick, but I needed to act. "Let's go see what he's doing out here," I said.

I ran to the stable with Billy close behind me and bridled the bay mare. Grabbing a handful of her mane, I swung onto her back and pulled Billy up behind me. As we headed toward the swimming hole, I let her gallop while I prayed.

Bart, his back toward us, stood next to Sheriff Packard's horse, looking up at the man and either talking or listening. When he heard us coming, he turned and waved. I stopped the mare a few yards from them. Sheriff Packard didn't smile, but he took off his hat.

"Good morning, Ruth, howdy, Billy," he said. "I was telling Bart I have business out this way. I heard you have company, so I was just checking to see if everything is all right."

I let out a breath that I didn't realize I had been holding. "We're obliged, Sheriff," I said. "A family stopped to rest themselves and their animals for a few days. They're moving on soon."

As we watched the sheriff ride away, Billy slid from the mare. I looked at the boys.

"Well," I said, "let's not do that again any time soon."

"The sheriff asked me if Pa minded having company," Bart said.

I leaned forward, and my heart began to race. "What did you tell him?" I asked.

Bart grinned. "I told him if Pa minded, he didn't say anything about it."

When we had stopped laughing, I said, "I reckon Jem will be riding in soon, so you two should haul your fish up to the house and clean them. We'll need your full attention when he gets here."

I let the mare walk back to the stable. As I turned her loose in the corral, I was still thanking God that Sheriff Packard had left. I hung up the bridle and walked back to the wash tubs. Sarah was kneeling in the spot where I had been. She pulled a shirt from the soapy water and began to wring it out.

"Sarah," I said, "isn't that the same shirt I was washing before I left?"

"It is," she said. "I don't reckon we'll get to that basket of clothes Mrs. Wells gave us," she said, "but our laundry sure will be clean!"

We finished our laundry, and I was fastening the last stocking to the clothesline when Sarah spotted Jem. We walked to where the boys were washing the cleaning table. Thad had returned from checking fences in time to help clean the last of the fish. He dumped a bucket of water on the table.

"I see him," he said. "With the Wells family sitting on the porch, I reckon we can start our performance as soon as Sheriff Jem gets here." He set the bucket on the ground under the table. "I've been praying all morning that this will work, and I know you have too," he said. He looked at Sarah, then at me. "Let's make it seem real."

"Act One, Scene Two," Sarah said.

Thad looked at the boys. "You ready?"

They nodded their heads, and we separated to take our places. Sarah walked to the clothesline and began to take down the clothes that were dry. She folded each item and placed it in a basket. I headed toward the house.

Mr. and Mrs. Wells sat in the chairs. Mr. Wells was smoking his pipe, and Mrs. Wells was reading one of our books. The older children sat on the bench, either reading our books or drawing in our sketch pads.

As I stepped onto the porch, Mrs. Wells spoke without looking at me. "The children are hungry," she said, "and so are Paul and I."

I smiled at her. "I was just getting ready to—" I looked at Jem and made myself stop smiling.

"What's wrong?" asked Mrs. Wells.

"Nothing—I hope," I said. As I stepped off the porch and walked out to meet Jem, I was smiling. "Nothing for me, I reckon," I whispered. "Help us get this right, Lord."

CHAPTER 16

Being the nosy people they were, I reckoned Mr. and Mrs. Wells would follow me so that they could hear what Jem and I were saying. Sure enough, they trailed along behind me. Jem stepped down, removing his hat and smiling at me. Billy and Bart led his horses to the trough for some water. The performance had begun. I reminded myself that, if we could, we wanted to fool the Wells family without lying to them.

"Howdy, Jem," I said. "Did you have any trouble herding those rustlers to jail?"

"No, Ma'am," he said. "They won't be rustling anybody's cattle for a long time."

Thad had been splitting firewood behind the house. He walked to where we stood, took off his gloves, and shook hands with Jem.

"Howdy, Jem," he said. "What brings you out this way? Are you trailing outlaws?"

Bart and Billy had tied Jem's horses to the hitching rail near the stable after giving them water. They wandered over to join us.

"Howdy, Thad," Jem said. "As a matter of fact, I'm trailing a couple of hombres who ambushed a miner a few days ago. They beat him up pretty bad and stole his poke— about $400 in gold dust."

"We don't want to keep you from doing your job," I said. "I was just getting ready to feed everybody—oh, I'm sorry—I forgot my manners! These folks stopped to rest themselves and their animals for a few days—Kate and Paul Wells."

Sarah had finished folding our clean clothes and walked over to join us. "I'm taking these clothes into the house," she said. "I can help you get the food ready. Can you stay long enough to eat something, Jem?"

"Well," Jem said, "I didn't just stop here to water my horses. I need to talk to y'all about something important."

"Come inside then," I said. "You and the boys wash up first. Then you can sit at the table, have some coffee, and talk to us while Sarah and I get your food ready. Will that work?"

Jem smiled. "I reckon it will," he said.

Mr. and Mrs. Wells followed Sarah and me as far as the porch. Without speaking, they sat on the chairs. I reckoned they wanted to hear what Jem had to tell us just as much as we wanted them to hear it.

Sarah whispered, "Act One went well. Here goes Act Two!" I felt a knot in my stomach as I whispered a prayer for help.

Jem and the boys walked in a few minutes later. Jem started to close the door; but when he looked at me, I shook my head. Leaving it partially open, he walked to the table and sat. Since Sarah and I were working on the other side of the room from the table, I reckoned raising my voice wouldn't seem odd to the Wells family.

"What can we do for you, Jem?" I asked. Although the Wells family couldn't see us, we had decided we'd sound more believable to them if we acted out our roles as we talked.

Jem rested both elbows on the table and put his head in his hands. He waited for a minute before he replied. He sat up and shook his head slowly as he looked at each of us.

"I don't want to have this conversation," he said, "but somebody has to say something. I reckon it's my job." He looked at Thad. "How long has your pa been dead?" he asked.

Thad looked at me, then turned to Jem. "What are you talking about?" Thad asked.

"I haven't seen him for more than a month," Jem said. "Y'all have come up with some pretty good excuses to explain his absence, but I wasn't born yesterday."

"We already knew that," Billy said. "I'm the youngest one here, and I wasn't born yesterday!"

"Billy," I said, "hush!"

"The thing is," Jem said, "when folks around here find out your pa's gone, they'll be worried about you, and they won't stand for leaving you five children alone on this ranch."

"We're not children," I said. "At least, some of us aren't." I was pacing back and forth as I talked. "This ranch belongs to us. What could they do?"

"They'd come out here with a buckboard," Jem said. "They'd load you and some of your things into it and take you to an orphanage in Tucson."

I nodded at Billy. He had been waiting for his turn.

"No!" he screamed. "I ain't going to no orphan home!"

I pointed at the door, and Billy took off at a dead run. I glanced at Sarah.

"Billy!" she yelled, "Come back!" Then she turned to Bart, who still sat at the table, grinning. "Bart, go get him!" He jumped from his chair and ran out the door.

Sarah stood by the sideboard while I continued to pace back and forth. Jem and Thad still sat at the table. We waited without speaking for a few minutes, and then someone tapped on the door.

"Come in," Thad said.

As Mr. Wells opened the door, I looked as worried as I could. Sarah wiped her eyes on her apron and sniffed before turning away from the door.

"May I be of some assistance?" he asked.

"No—but thank you," I said. "We'll call you when dinner is ready."

He smiled and stepped onto the porch. No one was surprised when he left the door ajar.

Thad smiled and nodded toward me. I took a deep breath.

"Jem," I said, "besides you, who knows Pa is dead?"

Jem stroked his moustache. "I don't reckon anybody does. Why are you asking?"

I stopped pacing and faced Jem. "Pa's been gone for more than two months, but you're the only person who knows he's gone. We planned to keep his passing a secret because we want to live here and run this ranch. We don't want to move to an orphanage." I walked to the table, poured more coffee, and sat across from Jem.

"You've been all over our property in the past month," I said. "Does the ranch look like it's being run well?"

"It does," he said.

"It should," I said. "Thad, Sarah, and I have been running it for the past year without much help from Pa, and for the past two months without any help."

Sarah walked to the table and, smiling, set a plate of biscuits between us. Thad and Jem each took one.

"Are you worried about us, Jem?" I asked.

Jem finished chewing a mouthful of biscuit and took a sip of coffee. "I don't follow you, Ruth," he said.

"You said folks will be worried about us when they find out we're living here without our parents," I said. "Do you think we're in danger?"

Jem dunked a piece of biscuit in his coffee and ate it. "I do not," he said.

Sarah set a bowl of dried beef and beans in front of each of us and then handed us spoons. Jem leaned forward to smell the beans. He closed his eyes, licked his lips, and smiled.

"What about the way we're running the ranch?" I asked. "Are we keeping things in good shape?"

Jem was blowing on a spoonful of beans to cool them off. "I told you this place looks good," he said. "Neither the house nor the stable needs repairs as far as I can tell. The fences look good, and your stock looks healthy." He put the beans into his mouth and nodded his approval at Sarah and me as he chewed.

"Ruth is almost sixteen," Thad said, "and I'll be fifteen in a few months. I reckon we can run this place as well as any grown folks could." He dipped a biscuit in his beans, pushed it into his mouth, and licked his fingers.

"I can't argue with you on that count," Jem said. "You don't seem to need anybody's help."

I swallowed a spoonful of beans. They really were delicious. I took a sip of coffee.

"Jem," I said, "do you mean that you don't aim to pack us off to the orphanage, now that you know Pa is dead?"

Even though nobody from the Wells family could see him, Jem gave me a confused look. "Now, why would I do that?"

I heard someone on the porch gasp. Then Mr. and Mrs. Wells were talking, but we couldn't make out what they were saying. I pushed back from the table, crossed the room, and put my empty bowl in the dish pan. Then I started toward the door. I didn't even try to hide my smile. Thad and Sarah were right behind me.

"Curtain call," Sarah whispered.

CHAPTER 17

Mr. and Mrs. Wells were standing when we walked onto the porch. The look on their faces told me they knew what was coming.

"I reckon you can feed the young'uns, Mrs. Wells," I said, "while your husband hitches the team to your wagon. He can eat when he's finished, and then you folks can be on the road."

"We planned to leave at sunup," she said.

"You're burning daylight," I said. "You have two hours."

"I'll give Mr. Wells a hand," Thad said. "I reckon we can have them ready to leave in *one* hour."

"I'm obliged for the help," Mr. Wells said, "but I don't know why you'd offer."

"Two reasons," Thad said. "First, I want you folks out of here as soon as you can be." Thad's hat had been hanging down his back on its stampede string. He reached over his shoulders, grabbed it by its brim, and put it on his head. "Second," he said, "I want to make sure none of our belongings end up in your wagon." Before Mr. Wells could reply, Thad turned and walked toward the corral.

"Somewhere along the way," Sarah said from close behind me, "I reckon our brother grew into a man."

I turned around and hugged her. "I reckon he did," I said.

"I don't understand why they're leaving," Billy said. "They told Bart and me they'd stay as long as they wanted to."

We were sitting on the porch, watching the Wells family's wagon drive away. It grew smaller and smaller until it finally disappeared in the cloud of dust it was raising.

"Pretend that one day, Thad and I go for a ride," I said.

"Where are you going?" Billy asked.

"I don't know," I said, "somewhere three hours away."

"I want to go too," Billy said.

"Billy," I said, "we're pretending. While we're gone, you get Pa's old pistol and accidentally shoot one of our sheep." I saw tears in Billy's eyes. "We're just pretending," I said.

Billy wiped his sleeve across his eyes. I tried hard not to smile.

"Bart sees you shoot the sheep, and he gets an idea," I said. "He tells—"

"Why can't Bart shoot the sheep and I get the idea?" Billy asked.

"Bart's idea is a bad one," I said. "Keep listening, and you'll see." I had to look away when Billy narrowed his eyes and stuck out his bottom lip.

"Bart tells you that he won't say anything, and he'll help you bury the sheep where Thad and I won't find it. If he does that for you, you have to do all his chores for a month."

Bart had been sitting on a bench with his brothers, but he jumped up and took a step toward me. "I wouldn't do that to Billy!" he said.

Thad grabbed the back of Bart's shirt and sat him down again. Putting his arm around Bart's shoulder, Thad said, "We're pretending—remember?"

"Billy, what could you do to keep from having to do Bart's chores for a month?"

Billy thought for a minute and then turned to grin at Bart.

"I'd help Bart dig the hole for the sheep," he said. "After we threw the sheep into the hole, I'd shoot Bart and throw him in the hole too. Then I'd bury both of them!"

"Billy Martin! What a horrible thing to say!" This time I was the one who was standing.

Billy was still grinning, and so were Thad, Bart, and Sarah.

"You said we was only pretending," Billy said. Sarah giggled, and then all of us were laughing.

I sat down and tried again. "Billy," I said, "Bart could make you do anything as long as he knew your secret and we didn't. Without shooting him, how could you take away his power over you?"

Billy took off his hat and scratched his head. "I don't know, Ruth," he said.

Bart grinned. "I reckon I might," he said.

"Go ahead," I said.

He looked at Billy. "I could only make you do my chores if Thad and Ruth didn't know about the sheep," he said.

Billy looked confused. "Only you and me know about the sheep, right?" he asked.

"Yep," Bart said, "and I ain't going to tell them because I want you to keep doing my chores."

Billy grinned. "I'd have to tell on myself!" he said. "Then Bart couldn't make me do anything!"

"That's what we did with the Wells family, isn't it?" Sarah asked. "They made us let them stay here by threatening to tell the sheriff that Pa is dead. When the sheriff found out about Pa, they couldn't control us anymore. They had to leave."

"The thing is," Thad said, "we made the Wells family *think* the sheriff found out about Pa being dead. I reckon our plan worked fine, thanks to Jem; but he rode away right after the Wells family left, and now we still have to deal with Sheriff Packard, the *real* sheriff."

"I reckon if Sheriff Packard ever finds out about Pa being gone," Sarah said, "he won't be as understanding as Sheriff Jem was."

Thad laughed and shook his head. "I don't reckon he will," he said. "We just need to make sure he *doesn't* find out." He looked at each of us. "That means we need to keep doing what we've been doing."

"And try to do it even better," I said. "We have to put on a show for the sheriff—and anybody else who calls on us—the way we did for the Wells family."

"Did we lie to Mr. and Mr. Wells?" Bart asked.

"I don't reckon we did," Thad said. "They stuck their noses into our business, watched us, and made their own decisions. We didn't tell them anything that wasn't true, did we?"

No one answered, but all of us shook our heads. Thad stood and stepped to the edge of the porch.

"I don't reckon anybody is fixin' to stop by and offer to do our chores for us," he said, "so we'd best get busy. We're burnin' daylight."

I stood beside Sarah with my arm around her shoulders, watching the boys walk toward the stable. "We're moving back into our house," I said, "after we give it a good cleaning."

Sarah slipped her arm around my waist and hugged me. "Yes," she said. She sniffed the air and then wrinkled her nose. "It smells like Wells." We were both laughing as we turned and walked into the house.

That evening at dinner, Thad's prayer was a little longer than usual. He thanked God for delivering us from the Wells family and for giving us Jem as a friend. Then he asked God to take care of us, to help us work the ranch and protect our secret. He ended his prayer by thanking God for the food and making a final request.

"And, Lord," he said, "please help us make You and Ma proud of us. Amen."

"Amen," the rest of us said.

We ate venison stew and corn bread—the same meal we had eaten many other times. But as I looked at Sarah and my brothers that night, I couldn't remember a time when it had tasted so good.

CHAPTER 18

Keeping Pa's death a secret was our most important concern, but it wasn't our only concern. Running the ranch kept all five of us busy most days. We tried to set aside some time each Sunday for hymn singing, Bible reading, and rest. Sometimes we succeeded; sometimes we didn't.

The Sunday after we'd chased off the Wells family, Thad and I sat on the porch, drinking coffee. The day was warm, but a cool breeze blew along the porch. I was leaning back in my chair, half asleep, when Thad spoke.

"Sometimes I feel like we're in the swimming hole, treading water," he said.

I sat up, shaking my head to clear it. "What do you mean?" I asked. I leaned to my right, picked up my cup from the floor, and drank some lukewarm coffee.

"If you're treading water in the deep part of the swimming hole where you can't touch bottom," he said, "what happens when I throw one of your boots to you and you catch it?"

"Why would you do that?" I asked.

"I have no idea why," he said, "but pretend I did. What would happen to you?" He stood, picked up the coffee pot, stepped toward me, and filled my cup. After filling his own cup and putting the pot down, he returned to his chair.

"I reckon I'd sink," I said.

Holding his cup in his right hand, he pointed at me with his left trigger finger. "And that's where we are with the ranch," he said.

"Have you eaten some loco weed?" I asked. "You're not making a bit of sense."

Thad leaned back in his chair, looked at the porch roof, and sighed. "I'm sorry," he said. "Let me try again." He drank some coffee and then leaned forward, resting his elbows on his knees while he held his cup in both hands.

"I reckon we're doing a pretty good job of running the Box M," he said, "but it's taking everything each of us can do." He sat up and drank some coffee, then leaned forward again. "What happens if one of us gets hurt or sick? What happens if someone steals our herd?"

"You mean," I said, "what happens if we're in the swimming hole and someone throws us a boot?"

Thad grinned. "You catch my drift!" he said.

"I do now," I said. I drank some coffee. "What can we do?"

"I don't know," Thad said, "but we need some kind of a plan. How much money do we have?"

"Ninety-seven dollars," I said. "The same forty-seven dollars we've in the Arbuckles' Bank for close to a year, plus the fifty Jem gave us."

The Arbuckles' Bank was a coffee bag that held all the cash money we had. Ma had saved the empty bag six or seven years ago and had started hiding inside it whatever money came her way. She kept the bag in plain sight on a shelf in the kitchen, one shelf above a bag that looked the same but really had coffee in it. I don't reckon Ma was trying to hide the money from Pa because she didn't trust him. She told me once that she believed having a little money tucked away to cover "unexpected expenses" was just a good idea. Although she had never said so, I reckoned she was better at saving money than Pa was.

"That's all we have?" Thad asked. He sighed. "I don't reckon that'll help us much if—no—*when* we have to start repairing or replacing things around here."

"That money has lasted," I said, "because we can do most of the work that needs done around here. We can barter for the things we can't grow or build ourselves."

Thad smiled at me. "I'm sorry, Ruth," he said. "I know you're right, and I know we have God watching over us too." He drank the last of his coffee and stood. "I reckon I just get discouraged sometimes when I think about how much Pa used to do that I can't."

I stood, and we hugged each other. "We can do this," I said. "The young'uns are watching us, and they'll follow our example."

Sarah had been reading in the parlor. She stepped through the doorway and stretched. "Any coffee left?" she asked.

Thad stooped to pick up the pot. "I'm sorry, Sarah," he said. "I reckon we drank it."

Sarah took the pot from Thad and smiled. "You don't look sorry," she said. "I'll add some beans and boil another pot."

Thad and I walked across the yard to the corral. The bay mare stood against the fence, and Thad patted her neck. He jerked his hand away and then tapped his fist on the top rail of the fence. "I'd almost forgotten," he said. I was standing beside him, and he turned to face me. "Jem said he'd be back in a few days to bring us our share of the reward for the rustlers. He didn't want to mention the money in front of the Wells family. He had business to tend to, so he said he'd be back."

"Did he say how much our share is?" I asked.

"Nope," Thad said, "and I didn't ask."

"Anything will help," I said.

We talked for a while, walking around the corral and the stable before returning to our chairs on the porch. We had been sitting there for a few minutes when Sarah stepped onto the porch with a cup in each hand and a grin on her face. Thad and I accepted the coffee and thanked her. She walked to a bench and sat, looking at me and still grinning.

"What are you grinning for?" I asked.

Thad had been about to taste his coffee, but he lowered his cup. "You'd better not have put something in our coffee," he said.

Sarah giggled. "There's nothing wrong with your coffee," she said. "I'm just enjoying a special occasion."

"What have you done?" I asked. All three of us were grinning now.

"Oh, I haven't done anything, Ruth," she said. She giggled again. "This time *you've* done something. You know how you scold me when I don't put something back where I got it?"

Sarah was enjoying herself so much that Thad and I couldn't help but smile. "All right," I said, "once for me and a hundred times for you—*if* you're right and I really didn't put something back where it belongs."

"I was making coffee," she said, "when I noticed that you didn't put back—of all things—the Arbuckles' Bank!"

As a little girl, I had made the mistake of running up behind a neighbor's pony. I had spooked the pony, and it had kicked me in the stomach. I had that same feeling as I realized what Sarah had said. Without speaking, I looked first at Thad and then back at Sarah. She had stopped grinning, and she shook her head slowly. "Oh, no," she said.

"Ruth," Thad said, "You're the only one of us who handles that money, and I don't reckon you'd forget to put it back."

"I haven't touched it except to add the fifty dollars from Jem," I said. "I took the bag from the shelf, added the money, and put the bag back where it belongs." I stood and walked into the house. As I passed Sarah, I tried to smile at her. "No offense intended," I said.

She wiped a tear away with the back of her hand. "None taken," she said. "Go ahead and look."

I looked at each shelf in the pantry, not because I doubted Sarah, but because I had to see for myself that the money was gone before I could believe it.

"I don't reckon Bart and Billy knew the money was there," Thad said. "If they had found it, they'd have let us know."

"Mrs. Wells didn't lift a finger to help with the cooking while she was here," Sarah said, "but I reckon she and her husband looked through the whole house— including the pantry— searching for anything that had value. If we look closely enough, we'll likely find other things missing too." She pulled out a chair and sat with her elbows on the table, her head in both hands.

Thad had been sitting at the other end of the table. He stood, pushed in his chair, and started toward the parlor. At the doorway, he stopped and turned to look at me. "I'd be obliged if you'd pack me a couple days' worth of trail grub," he said.

When he walked into the kitchen again a few minutes later, he carried his rifle and wore Pa's old cap-and-ball revolver in a holster at his waist. A chill ran down my spine.

"Where are you going?" I asked.

"To get back what belongs to us," he said. "I'll take the Buckskin. I should be able to catch up with them by sundown tomorrow—if not, then early the next morning."

I was scared and angry. "And when you catch up with them," I said, "you reckon they'll tell you how sorry they are, and they'll give back our money?"

Thad grinned. "I reckon they'll give back our money and anything else they stole," he patted the rifle, "if I ask them the right way. As for saying they're sorry, I was planning to tell them that myself."

"It's not worth the risk!" I said. "If anything goes wrong, you could wind up—"

Bart and Billy burst through the doorway. "Look what we got!" Billy said. Each of them held one end of a dead rattlesnake that looked to be at least six feet long. Both boys knew that they were supposed to keep clear of rattlers—even small ones. I was ready to start a serious scolding when Thad spoke. I put both hands on my hips and glared at him, but he grinned.

"That's a fine rattler," he said. "What do you aim to do with it?"

The excitement on the boys' faces almost made me forget that I was angry with them.

"First, we're going to skin it!" Bart said.

"Then," Billy said, "we're going to cook it and eat it!" Both boys grinned when Sarah and I showed our disgust.

"I can't help but notice," Thad said, "that this critter's dead. How did he wind up that way? Which one of you killed him, and who's going to skin him and cook him?"

"He's getting heavy," Billy said. He looked at Bart. "Let's put him on the table."

Although Thad had been doing the talking, my hands were still on my hips as I stepped between the boys and the table. "Think again, Mister," I said. "The only table you'll put that snake on is the fish cleaning table. Turn around and march back outside. We'll follow you so you can finish telling your story."

Thad grabbed the snake in the middle and helped the boys lay it on the table. Both Bart and Billy were sweating and breathing hard. "We carried him all the way from the swimming hole," Bart said.

"I want to hear how this snake came to be dead," I said. My hands rested on my hips again, but neither boy looked worried. In fact, both of them were still grinning. Both started talking at the same time.

"Whoa!" I said. "One at a time, please. Bart, you're older; tell us what happened."

"I want to tell what happened," Billy said. He sniffed and wiped tears away with his sleeve.

Bart looked at him and then back at me. He shrugged his shoulders and grinned. "Let Billy tell it," he said. "I'll speak up if he forgets something."

"Thank you, Bart," I said. "I'm proud of you. Billy, go ahead; tell us what happened."

Billy swallowed hard and wiped his eyes with his sleeve again. "Me and Bart was fishing, but we wasn't catching anything," he said. "So we put rocks on our poles to keep fish from pulling them in if they got hooked while we wasn't looking." Billy was grinning again.

"We circled the swimming hole three times, getting farther and farther away each time."

Bart, who stood a little behind Billy, grinned at me and held up four fingers. I looked at the ground so Billy wouldn't see my smile.

"As we walked up to them rocks on the far side of the swimming hole—" Billy grabbed the snake's tail and shook it. "We heard *this*!"

"You'd best be getting ready to tell us that you ran away," I said.

"We started to," Billy said, "but then he pinned that snake's head with the butt of his rifle, pulled out that big knife and—" Billy made a chopping motion with his hand at the other end of the snake. "He whacked its head clean off!"

Sarah, Thad, and I looked at each other, then at Bart.

"Don't look at me," he said. "I don't own a rifle or a big knife."

"Your story," Thad said, seems to have a mighty big hole in it. One of you needs to fill it in by telling us who else was down at the swimming hole with you."

"Howdy, Folks. I reckon that'd be me," said Jem.

Sarah let out a yelp, and so did I. Thad even jumped. Bart and Billy laughed because they had seen Jem coming up behind us.

"I'm sorry if I startled you," Jem said. "I wasn't trying to sneak up on you; I reckon I'm just used to moving quietly."

Sarah smiled at Jem. "No hard feelings," she said. "I'm sure we'll recover from the scare in an hour or two." We all laughed.

"Would you like some coffee?" I asked. "I have a few biscuits left from breakfast too, if you're hungry."

Jem smiled. "I reckon I'm always hungry for those biscuits," he said. "Let me show your brothers how to get this snake ready to cook, and then I'll come in for coffee."

"If you don't need my help," Sarah said, looking at me, "I'd like to learn how to cook one of these critters too."

I smiled. "You just have at it, Sarah," I said. "You can be our rattlesnake cook from now on."

CHAPTER 19

"I came back for two reasons—well, maybe three," Jem said. He took a bite from the biscuit he was holding, closed his eyes, and smiled while he chewed it. He drank some coffee and then looked around the table at each of us.

"Doing the kind of work I do," he said, "teaches a man to read people. It teaches a man to trust his gut too." He ate more of his biscuit and washed it down with coffee. "I knew Mr. and Mrs. Wells weren't right as soon as I laid eyes on them. When they left here, my gut told me to follow them." He put the last bite of his biscuit into his mouth, chewed for a minute, and swallowed it. I poured him more coffee. He took a sip, set his cup on the table, and took another biscuit from the plate in front of him.

"Since they think I'm the sheriff," he said, "I acted like one. I told them that some of your possessions had turned up missing and that I needed them to check their wagon to see if their children might have picked up a couple of your things by mistake." He bit into the biscuit and smiled at me.

"They checked just because you asked them to?" I asked.

"Well," Jem said, "I may have mentioned that if they didn't do as I asked, I'd bring them back here so that all of us could search their wagon."

"Did they give you anything?" Thad asked.

"They only confessed to taking some food," Jem said, "but they'd already eaten most of it." Jem smiled. "Judging by the weight of this bag, I reckon they used most of your coffee too; but I brought this back anyway." He pulled a packet from one of the pockets in his duster and slid it across the table to me. "Might be enough left in here for another cup or two," he said. It was a flattened Arbuckles' Coffee bag.

My hands shook as I opened the bag and counted out ninety-seven dollars on the table.

"Ruth," Billy whispered, "are you crying because somebody put money in a coffee bag?"

"No, Billy," I said. I wiped away the tears with the back of my hand, but I couldn't stop more from coming. "This is all the money we have, and we hid it in this bag. Mr. and Mrs. Wells found it and stole it, but—" I couldn't go on, so I nodded at Thad.

"Mr. and Mrs. Wells stole it," he said, "but Jem made them give it back to us." Thad wiped his sleeve across his eyes and then spoke for all of us. "We're much obliged, Jem."

Jem smiled. "I reckon that's what friends are for," he said.

"That's all the money we have?" Bart asked.

I still couldn't speak. Sarah said, "Yes, it is."

"Well now," Jem said, "that's not quite all the money you have." He reached into the same pocket and pulled out a small leather pouch, fastened at the top with a drawstring. As he slid it across the table to me, he smiled again and said, "This is your share of the reward for helping me capture those three rustlers. I reckon you'll want to add it to your poke before you hide it away somewhere safe."

I had stopped crying, but I started again after I loosened the drawstring and dumped the contents of the pouch onto the table. It had contained five $20 gold coins—more money than any of us Martins had ever been paid before. Thad, Sarah, and I couldn't speak.

"That's a hundred dollars!" Bart said.

"I reckon we're filthy rich!" Billy said. "Jem, you got any more outlaws that need catching?"

Thad started laughing first, but the rest of us weren't far behind him. When the laughter stopped a few minutes later, Jem finished the biscuit he had been eating and drank the last of his coffee. He put his elbows on the table, folded his hands, and rested his chin on them.

"The answer to Billy's question is the third reason I came back here," he said.

Billy jumped off his chair and started to speak, but he looked at me and stopped. I motioned for him to sit and then put my finger to my lips.

"Shush, Billy," I said. "This is a time for listening, not talking." I smiled at Jem. "Go ahead," I said.

"I've been thinking about something ever since we met," he said. "For the past three years, I've been chasing outlaws all over the Arizona Territory. Sometimes I track them for two or three weeks before I catch up with them, and they run in every direction. My horse and pack horse are fine animals; but, sooner or later, they get plumb worn out."

Jem leaned back in his chair and folded his arms across his chest. "Do you know how the Pony Express worked—how those boys moved the mail across the country so fast?" he asked.

"They changed horses a lot," Thad said.

"Every ten to fifteen miles," Jem said. "Some outlaws have seen the wisdom of that practice," he said, "and they stash extra horses along their escape route. Since the lawmen—and bounty hunters like me—don't know the route the outlaws will take, we usually end up riding some tired horses."

"When are you going to answer my question?" Billy asked.

I looked across the table at Billy and shook my head. He folded his arms across his chest and stuck out his lower lip.

"I'll answer it now, Billy," Jem said. "Yes, there are other outlaws that you can help me catch—"

Billy sprang from his chair again. "I knew it—"

"Hold on, Billy," Jem said. "I wouldn't take any of you on the trail with me. It's too dangerous." He leaned forward, folded his hands, and let them rest on the table. "You can still help me catch outlaws though. I'd like to look through your horses. I want to buy two of them and leave them here. Your job will be to take care of them—I'll pay you for your work and for their food."

Thad was grinning. "You want relay horses!" he said.

"I do," Jem said. He leaned back in his chair and folded his arms again. "Not all outlaws will ride this way, but I reckon a bunch of them will. This part of the territory has a lot of places to hide."

"What exactly would you need from us?" I asked.

Jem was still leaning forward. "I'd need you to ride both horses to keep them in good shape," he said. He looked at Thad. "I noticed a forge in the lean-to behind the stable. Can you shoe the horses and keep their feet in good condition?"

Thad grinned. "I reckon I can," he said. "Pa taught me how. Anything else?"

"Not that I can think of," Jem said. "I'd like to ride out at sunup. Could I look at your herd now?"

"Let me saddle a horse," Thad said.

Sarah and I watched the two riders trot their horses toward the pasture. I turned to the boys and asked,

"Before you got mixed up with the rattlesnake, did you catch any fish?"

Bart and Billy looked at each other and then at me. "We left them on the stringer," Billy said.

Did you have enough for supper?" Sarah asked.

"I reckon not," Bart said, "but we can catch more. How much time do we have?"

I looked at Sarah. She shrugged her shoulders. "At least an hour," she said.

"An hour?" Bart asked. "With that much time, we'll have to throw half the fish we catch back in the water!"

When I snatched a frying pan from the stove and started toward them, the boys ran out the door, laughing. Sarah was laughing too. "We have time to make johnny cakes," she said.

"Then let's make some," I said.

That night after supper, the boys had gone outside, and Sarah was washing dishes. Jem and Thad sat at the table across from me. Jem spoke to both of us, but I let Thad answer him.

"I'll give you $200 for the buckskin and $150 for the black with the white blaze—she'll be my pack horse," Jem said. "I'll pay $20 for putting shoes on them, and $10 a month for taking care of them—riding, feeding, brushing—well, I reckon you know how to take care of a horse, judging by the way your stock looks. Does that sound fair to you? Talk it over if you need to; I can go out to the stable and spread my bedroll."

Thad looked at me, and I nodded. Thad held out his hand to Jem, who shook it. "We have a deal, Jem," he said.

The next morning, Jem swallowed his last bite of flapjack and finished his coffee.

"Would you like more of anything?" Sarah asked.

"My horse is already going to hate me for eating so much," he said. "Thank you, Ladies, for a delicious breakfast."

A few minutes later, we watched Jem tighten the girth on his saddle and then check the pack horse. Thad shook Jem's hand, but the rest of us hugged him before he swung into the saddle.

"Y'all be careful," he said. "I reckon I'll probably be back this way in a month or so—maybe sooner, depending on which way the outlaws I'm tracking decide to run." He looked down at us and smiled. "I'll keep y'all in my prayers."

"We'll pray for you too, Jem," I said. "*Vaya con Dios.*"

As we watched him ride away, I put one arm around Bart's shoulders and the other around Billy's. "We need to keep our promise and pray for him," I said. "I reckon Jem will likely face some real trouble before we see him again."

I didn't know it then, but before we saw Jem again, we'd face some real trouble too.

Thank you for reading this book. I hope you found it both interesting and enjoyable. Please take a few minutes to leave a review on Amazon.com, Goodreads, BookBub, Facebook, or Instagram.

You can also leave a comment or ask a question at www.marklredmond.com or email me at markredmond53@gmail.com. Photos of you holding a copy of one of my books are always welcome.

Check the next page for a list of all my books. If you visit my website and join my posse, I'll email you updates on new books as they're published; and I'll and share other things that are happening in my world. My posse is growing, but there's room for you!

Books by Mark L. Redmond

The Arty Anderson Series

Arty Goes West
Arty and the Hunt for Phantom
Arty and the Texas Ranger
Arty's Long Day
Arty and the Cattle Rustlers
Arty's Tough Trail

The Nate Landry Series

Bounty Hunter Nate Landry: Major Issues
Bounty Hunter Nate Landry: Family Fury

The Box M Series

The Box M Gang

Short Story Collections

Five for the Trail

CPSIA information can be obtained
at www.ICGtesting.com
Printed in the USA
JSHW021941250123
36833JS00002B/79